MUCKROSS ABBEY
and other stories

Also by Sabina Murray

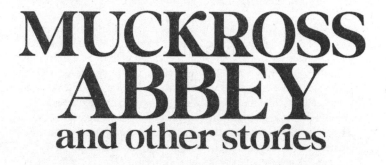

MUCKROSS ABBEY
and other stories

SABINA MURRAY

ILLUSTRATIONS BY GABRIEL HENNESSY

Black Cat
New York

FIRST EDITION

Published simultaneously in Canada
Printed in the United States of America

This book was set in 12-pt. Goudy Oldstyle
by Alpha Design & Composition of Pittsfield, NH.

First Grove Atlantic paperback edition: March 2023

Library of Congress Cataloging-in-Publication
data is available for this title.

ISBN 978-0-8021-5748-5
eISBN 978-0-8021-5749-2

Black Cat
an imprint of Grove Atlantic
154 West 14th Street
New York, NY 10011

Distributed by Publishers Group West

groveatlantic.com

23 24 25 26   10 9 8 7 6 5 4 3 2 1

For Nick and Gabe

Contents

———•———

The Long Story

A hiker lost on the moors. A cliché. The farmer had warned him that one got turned around, that he should head back to the village, that despite the bright sun that held when not completely blocked by sudden slabs of gray cloud, rain was a probability in the next couple of hours. Or fog. He'd thought the farmer was *taking the piss*, entertained by his American accent, his fancy boots, his raincoat made out of astronaut fabric. He'd kept going. And now it was just sheep, who had suddenly all turned in the same direction, presenting him with their backsides. A fox had hurried ahead, glancing over her shoulder with a cautioning look before disappearing into the steep, ascending spine of rock that rose up the sloping grass. The temperature was falling, and around the sun a fuzzy halo announced a change of weather. Fog had begun to form at the border of trees. He was alone, and the thought that he'd have to wait out the night filled him with a combination of embarrassment and awe. Why had he not listened? Startled, he heard a cough and, turning quickly, thought he saw a person—a tall figure in a black coat—but this figure, an illusion, was quickly erased by a wall of fog. The man had disappeared into it. "Hello?" he called. "Hello?"

But it was Dartmoor in an obscuring, earthbound cloud, embraced by one of its impenetrable, legendary mists. The rain had started to patter in. He could barely see three feet in front of him now and the only sound was that of a low wind, a sort of breathing, as if the moors were inhaling and exhaling, as if the moors themselves were alive. He felt a panic then. Sound carried strangely in the wet air. He stood still, listening intently. He wondered if he should stay in place, which was infinitely better than falling into some sort of ditch and spraining his ankle or running into a wild animal. *The Hound of the Baskervilles* came to mind. The situation was ridiculous. He'd felt, as a world traveler, that there was no possible danger to be had in any English-speaking country, particularly England, which appeared to be completely sliced up with highways and overrun with villages, where the trees stood shoulder to shoulder in marked-out woodlands, and the concept of "civilization" seemed to extend to an infinite number of things, weather included. But this was a foul, barbaric weather, a Precambrian mist that seemed to erase all of man's achievements.

He would turn back in the direction of the farm but was uncertain in which direction that was. He thumbed to the compass on his phone, but there was no signal. A few minutes earlier, there had been a signal. What had blocked it? *Pick a direction*, he told himself. *Pick a direction and begin walking.*

"Hello?"

A woman's voice. He froze. Some revenant fear from childhood made him pause. Who would be out in this weather?

"Hello?"

It was the woman again.

"Yes?" he responded. There was a brightening off to his right. "Hello! I'm over here!" He heard footsteps, a snapping branch, and began to make his way to the voice and to the light that, as he approached, was concentrating itself into a circle.

"Hello!"

"Hello!"

The light swung around a few times, then flared into his eyes, and behind it the woman was revealed. She was slight, black haired, middle-aged, and wearing a barn jacket. She gave him a quizzical look. "The American hiker," she said. She, too, was American, which was disorienting but also a comfort. "Are you lost?"

He fought the urge to say no. He didn't know why he should trust her. "Yes. I got turned around."

"Follow me. My house is just over there." She gestured, swinging the light off to the left.

"How did you find me?" he asked.

"Tom Barker, my neighbor, phoned to say you were headed my way. He worries about people wandering around in the fog. It can be dangerous." They trudged quickly along. "And I'm Olivia."

"Paul," he said.

How she found the path home was a mystery, but she did. She opened a low wooden gate and, after he stepped through, swung it shut. The cottage was low-slung with a thatched roof and two windows that because of the light blazing from within seemed to be staring out at him with yellow eyes. She opened the door and stepped in. "Come in. You must be frozen. And kick off your shoes. This is a shoe-free house."

He unlaced his boots and removed his coat, which crackled as he hung it on the hook in the hallway.

"Go sit by the stove," she said, inviting him into the low-ceilinged living room. "I can make tea, but I'm guessing you could use a whiskey."

"Thanks," he responded.

She disappeared into the kitchen. The smell of stewing meat hung in the air. He hoped she had enough for two. He looked at the two chairs set by the stove and decided on the red corduroy piece, which looked slightly less comfortable than the brown recliner, which he thought must be his host's regular chair. He stretched his feet toward the fire and flexed his toes, feeling the burn in his extremities as the chill slowly gave over to the warmth emanating from the flaming logs. He heard footsteps upstairs and wondered if that's where she kept the liquor, but suddenly she was at the threshold.

"Here," said the woman. She handed him a simple glass with a good portion of whiskey and settled into her chair with a drink of her own.

He took a sip as she sipped hers and they peered across the gulf between their glasses. "So, Paul," she said, "beyond getting lost on the moor and being rescued, what's your story?"

"My story?" It wasn't very interesting. "I'm a doctoral student in geology and my adviser loaned me out to a friend of his in the petroleum business. The company is based in London. I'm not much interested in academia, so I thought I'd look at industry." He left out the bit about the girlfriend, recently ex, who *was* interested in academia, in Oxford right now in an apartment that the two had intended to share over the summer. Why was she smiling at him that way? It was making him uncomfortable, as if she were anticipating his saying stupid things and he was fulfilling her expectations. "And what about your story?"

"Mine?" She shot up an eyebrow. " . . . I've been living in this house for five years, and I rather like it."

"Isn't it lonely?"

"No." She grew introspective. "I find it peaceful."

"There are other peaceful places." But as he said it, couldn't think of any. "So why . . . this place?" He was lost and wasn't sure where he was.

"Ah, short version, I've always liked Thomas Hardy."

"And the long version?"

The woman laughed. She got up from her chair. "Would you like some stew? It's mutton. That's what we eat around here. And in the spring, lamb."

*　*　*

The woman was in the kitchen producing a clatter of bowls and cutlery. He let his eyes wander around the room. There was a landscape, which looked a lot like the surrounding landscape and must have been intended for people who missed the outdoors when they went indoors. She had only one photograph and that was of a young man, around twenty, with thick black hair and an intense gaze. He was probably the woman's son. There was something disturbing about the photograph, but on closer inspection, he wasn't sure of the reason: the young man had an ironic expression, but that was expected of people that age. He wondered if he was going to have to spend the night here or if the woman had some other plan for him—a neighbor's barn perhaps—and how he could broach the topic without seeming to be making assumptions. And then she reappeared with two bowls of stew, each with a big spoon in it.

"Is that your son?" he asked, gesturing to the mantel.

"Yes. Bennett."

"He has quite a presence."

"It was often remarked on."

He was very hungry and took one spoonful of stew and then another. His need to eat had created a silence, and he realized that he was being impolite. "You were going to tell me the long story," he said.

"The long story?"

8

"Of how you came to live here."

"Right," she said. "Where to start?"

She gave him a long, cold look that took in his face and then slowly dismissed it. "Bennett was an actor." The wind picked up then, rattling the windows and setting some unseen branch to a rhythmic thumping. "He was preparing for a role."

He looked questioningly in her direction. She, too, seemed to be wondering about the impact of the son's acting on the current circumstance.

"I was still teaching, you see, and I came here to complete the final edits on a book."

"You're a writer?" he asked.

"An art historian."

"What was the book about?"

"My book was about the Manila galleons. I was writing on the transfer of aesthetic and medium from Spain to the Philippines to Mexico."

"This seems like an odd place to write about that topic."

"I had a grant. My publisher was in Cambridge, and it was a cheap place within striking distance. I was on sabbatical."

"And you stayed."

"That's still the short story." She smiled. "I thought you wanted the long story."

Just then, it sounded as if there were someone knocking on the door. He turned to look over his shoulder to the vestibule, but his host seemed disinclined to move. She settled in her chair and took another spoonful of stew.

"You've been very generous," he said. "But I'm worried I'm intruding."

"Oh no," the woman responded. "You're actually stuck here for the night."

"You don't mind?"

"No. It doesn't happen that often. And you seem more pleasingly subdued than some of the other ones."

"Thanks." His gratitude was tempered. "It's a beautiful house."

"Bennett wasn't sure about it. He thought it was cliché. The thatched roof. The sheep. It offended his sensibilities. And he thought the English were absurd."

"All of them?" He laughed.

"Oh yes. Bennett could sense them looking down their noses at him, and he would say, '1776.' Of course, they had no idea what he was talking about."

"1776? The American Revolution?"

She raised her eyebrows in the affirmative. "He was right, you know. It wasn't so much nationalism, because he hated America too, but a sort of mild outrage that the English seemed so unaware of a revolution that had formed the collective consciousness of the entire thinking world. Cambodian Socialists think about the American Revolution. Why would the English, who were participants, be so indifferent?"

He hadn't studied the Revolution since middle school. His memory summoned Paul Revere on his horse. "Your son was studying history?" he said.

"No. As previously mentioned, he was an actor."

"Yes. You did say that."

"I was here for a semester. Bennett had originally intended to spend his spring break with his father, but his father—That doesn't matter. Bennett was preparing for a role and thought that my quiet ways might not intrude on his work. And we were very close, Bennett and I. He found my presence soothing."

"Did something happen to your son?" he asked.

"Yes." Her stew was done, and she set the bowl aside. She looked up at the boy's picture with such longing that Paul felt a wash of panic. "And that is the long story."

"He was an actor?" he asked, although she'd already said as much twice.

"Bennett was in college. He did acting and playwriting. He was a very talented boy. One of his classmates had written a play that had been selected to be performed and Bennett had landed the lead role. Bennett was also working on a play, set just before the American Revolution. It had to do with the British occupation of Boston. It was called *Occupation*."

"Good title," he said, "and strange subject matter."

The woman smiled. "Bennett often took inspiration from history. He thought history was a way to escape writing about his family, which is what most of the other students wrote about. Family dramas were predictable. Bennett said, 'Not only is every happy family alike, but every unhappy family is also alike. You have the overweening parent, the anxious child, the weird aunt or uncle.' But he would have been happy to have landed a role in one of those dramas. Instead, his ambitious playwriting friend had composed a piece on authenticity, the authenticity of writing itself."

Paul nodded along, wondering how this tied in with the woman's move to England. His whiskey was finished, and she leaned over with the bottle, pouring another good portion.

"The play," she said, "mostly involved various aspects of sincerity: kindness, truth, desire interacting with Bennett, who was playing the Writer. His job was to exchange lines with the other actors as he developed an escalating cough. At the end of the play, he manages to cough up something, but the actual writer, as opposed to 'the Writer'"—she hooked her fingers to show the difference—"had yet to figure out what this something was. One possibility was postmodernism, another an innocent child, and both these options would be difficult to stage in a way that had the intended impact on the audience."

"And what was the intended impact?" he asked.

"That wasn't Bennett's problem. He just had to cough."
She finished her own glass and as the whiskey glugged to

top it, said, "And he was here to work on it. Do you know any actors?"

"No," he said. "I mostly know geologists."

"Well, actors are a strange lot. When Bennett was preparing for his role in *Proof*, he played the father, he based the character on my father, his grandfather. He started out with the slippers and then the voice. He mimicked my father's accent, old-world Boston, and he occupied that identity for several weeks. It was as if my father and my son were both there, one imposed upon the other. It looked like Bennett, but the voice and mannerisms were all my father's. After Bennett was done with the role, he shed my father completely. And he was my son again."

There was a moment's silence.

"Bennett asked me to cough. I did. He said my cough was flat, limited. He needed a better cough. I told him that this house was damp and he might develop one. He said a cottage cough wouldn't have the effect he needed. He was committed to the project, even though he doubted that his friend's play, still unfinished mind you, would amount to much. The performance would still be important. If he could nail the cough, the escalating cough, it would earn him accolades. And you are wondering what kind of accolades those might be, and yes, they might be slight, but when you are an artist, you exist within the execution of the particular action. You are your own judge and jury, at least when you're doing it well. He had to manage that cough for himself. It had to meet his standards, and those standards were high. And as a true artist, he would sacrifice nothing to reach the closest approximation of the perfect escalating cough."

The woman had clearly been an indulgent mother, or perhaps this weirdness was just the effect of grief or the aftereffect of it, her dealing with loss.

"You don't know actors," she said with warmth. "Bennett worked on his cough and memorized lines. He was writing the first act of his play. I went through my galleys."

"Your galleon galleys?"

"Yes. They needed a lot of work. Bennett memorized lines and chatted online with his director as they tried to figure out how the play would end. And he worked on the cough. He coughed around the house. He began taking long walks."

"It is good walking country."

"As long as you respect the mists." She smiled. "They hide all manner of things."

"I thought I saw someone," he said. "But I lost him in the fog. He seemed to disappear."

"Or did disappear. Everything does. That is the function of time, to rob, to make things disappear, and without time, everything is still there, isn't it? The trick to keeping things is to find that pocket in reality where time doesn't hold effectively, where it slips or overlaps."

"Sure," he said. "That's in time theory, right?"

"It is a theory that involves time. And who knows how effective it is? Even Einstein was not convincing on time or couldn't make it line up with perceived reality." The woman shrugged. "Or perhaps your man just wandered off. The moors are lonely, but there have to be people to notice the fact of it for this to register. Some of us just like the empty places, but as we notice them, we displace their peaceful grandeur. Man corrupts everything. Places can be lonely with animals, the kestrels, the badgers, the foxes and ponies. But put a man there, and it's all destroyed. You become an eyesore for other men who wish to be alone, and they for you."

He wondered about his own presence on the moors.

"At least that's what Bennett thought. I would sit at that desk right there"—she gestured over his shoulder—"and do my edits. And Bennett would walk the moors. And one day, I saw him out there with a tall man in a long black coat. They were far off, but I knew it was Bennett—he had an odd loping walk—and this man was walking along with him. I found it strange, but why? Perhaps because the man didn't look like a farmer. He wasn't dressed that way. When I asked Bennett about it later, he said there had been no man."

"That's strange."

"Yes, I thought so. When I asked my neighbor Tom, you know him, he said that the description fit any number of people. He said the person I should be asking was my son, for weren't they walking together? But Bennett was adamant. And busy. He was still working on the cough but had also found sudden inspiration for his own play. He divided his hours between his work on *Occupation*, sitting at his computer, and working on his role as the Writer. He stood before the mirror in the hallway and coughed and coughed, delivered lines, and coughed, and then he would return to his computer. I thought he was working too hard, but I wasn't sure what else there was to do around here. And then once when he was standing before the mirror I heard him say, 'If I had seen that, I could make something really great.' I thought it was a line, but then I heard a reply. God knows where it came from—it was a raspy voice that responded—but then it was cut off by coughing. That coughing was a brutal, lung-crushing thing. It couldn't have come out of Bennett. I jumped from this chair and ran into the hall, and there was Bennett, calming the cough, covering his mouth. 'Are you all right?' I asked. And he responded, 'I am mastering the cough.' And I said something glib like, 'Just make sure it doesn't master you.'"

"We'd only been in the house a couple of weeks, and Bennett was becoming withdrawn. He'd always been eager to share work. I didn't have to ask. But he wasn't talking about his progress with the role, and he hadn't even mentioned his play. Dinner was chitchat about the news, rising British isolationism, but even on this issue, he was quiet where he had once been vociferous to the point of ridiculousness. I suggested a trip to the pub. We drove the five miles in. So, beer and pie and a change of scenery. I thought that Bennett should get out of the house, and he was amenable. We got into the car and drove to the village. I remember it was raining. The windows fogged up. Obscured vision is such an issue around here." She laughed and then grew quiet.

"But you made it."

"Oh, yes, Bennett and I. He ordered sausages. I don't know why I remember that, but I do. There were some old photographs hanging on the walls. One was of some local boys who had gone off to fight in the Great War. Bennett said, 'Not all of them came back,' which I thought was an odd thing to say. I responded, 'Regardless, they're all dead,' or something like it. And he followed it up with, 'Well, America took their time showing up for that one.' Of course, this surprised me. Bennett was usually so anti-English, and even if he did believe such a thing, he would have found a more reasoned way to express it. Also, to my knowledge he'd never studied World War I. I asked him what was informing his opinion."

"What did he say?"

"We were interrupted by one of the locals, who'd had more than his share of drink, and he asked us if we were the Americans renting the house. He asked us what we thought of it, and when he saw Bennett studying the photograph, he pointed out one of the men and said that his family were the ones who owned it, although now we were in touch with the grandniece. We drove home late that afternoon and Bennett went straight to his computer and I to my galleys. Late that evening, I asked if I could see what he had written. He usually shared his work with me. He said it was too early for him to show. I said something about the American Revolution, and he said he'd changed his mind. He was writing about the Great War, about a group of young men, some as young as seventeen, who had signed up from the town and gone to fight. He found the inspiration of the area too pervasive to ignore. He told me, 'The Somerset Light Infantry was present at all the major battles. Men from this very town were fighting in Flanders.' And I said, 'Flanders? Bennett, don't you mean Belgium?'"

"What's the difference?" he asked.

"Americans don't say 'Flanders.' Do you say 'Flanders'?"

"No," he replied. But then he rarely said "Belgium."

"Bennett thought for a minute. His response was interesting. He said that writing was a form of acting where you had to occupy each role, prepare for it from a state of being, that you, as a playwright, had to perform each of the roles in your head and then transcribe them in order for other people to constitute that identity into a living and breathing person. He had to be all the characters in his play, and his characters said 'Flanders.'"

"You think a lot about writing for someone who's an art historian," said Paul.

"More of an independent scholar, at this point." The woman nodded sagely. "I originally studied painting. My first love was the work of the Filipino painter Juan Luna. His masterpiece was *Spoliarium*, which depicts dead gladiators being stripped of their finery. Juan Luna was a revolutionary and the savage gladiators forced to bloody deaths to entertain their enslavers resonated with him. He occupied the bodies of each of the gladiators, breathed a death into each figure that whispered of an extinguished life. I am not an artist, but I understand the artist's need to inhabit. Much is written about Juan Luna and the painters of that era, which is why I moved on to other art forms."

"The Manila galleons."

"Yes. The stuff that circulated. I studied materials, specific patterns of embroidery . . . lesser arts. But the women who wrought those fine handkerchiefs lost their sight to create objects of such beauty that they seemed not to have been made by human hands but by some sort of magic. And the sight sacrificed to those stitches shone out of the fabric, forcing others to be awed by the impossible workmanship that had called those fine linens into being. Art is selfish and enslaves all of its true practitioners. If the possibility of a fine execution presents itself, the artist cannot fight it. The artist is helpless to the calling. Bennett could not resist the demands of his art."

Paul looked back to Bennett's picture. Although not more than twenty, he did not look helpless but rather seemed to have a powerful sense of purpose.

"One night, I was reading by the fire and fell asleep. When I awoke, the house was quiet, the fire just glowing embers, emptying the last of its heat into a cold room. I headed for bed, shutting off the lamp. The light in the kitchen was on, throwing off a muted brightness. I was not fully awake, perhaps, but as I passed the mirror in the hallway, the one that Bennett stood before to practice his lines, I was sure I saw a man within it. It was not my reflection, nor any reflection at all, but a figure peering out as if trapped behind the glass. He was taller than Bennett and quite gaunt. My hand went quickly for the hall switch, and, with that brighter light, the figure disappeared. But I saw him. I did. And I felt that Bennett, although he would not share it with me, had seen him too."

She reached out the bottle and he his glass, and she poured.

"Bennett's cough was improving, or worsening, depending on how you view it. Despite the fact that he was pleased with its progress, I was growing concerned. I tried to stay bright and supportive. I asked him if he and the director had found a way to end the play, and he made a joke that 'the end would find them.'"

"That's not a very funny joke."

"No. And the next day Bennett collapsed. I rushed him to the doctor in town. He was coughing up gallons of fluid. No one had seen anything like it. His lungs were full and he was drowning. My darling boy. He couldn't breathe. He held my hand and looked at me with desperate eyes, but near the end, those same eyes filled with conviction. He said, 'This is how the play ends.' 'How, my love?' I asked. 'How does the play end?' And he said, 'Not the shelling, not the machine guns, but me. I will cough up myself, man destroying himself. I will cough up man.'"

Outside, in the dark of night, a lone sheep was bleating sickly. It marked the time. Something shifted in the fire, signaling another moment. Paul felt . . . what was it? Inadequate, somehow, to the moment. He thought that perhaps he should offer a word of condolence, but the sense he got from this woman was fierce, maternal, loving pride.

"They said it was pneumonia." She wrinkled her nose, shook her head as if shaking off the thought. "Doctors. They labor and thrive in the darkness of our ignorance, ignorance of our own bodies. Bennett was rushed by ambulance to the hospital in Bristol and lasted two days there."

"He died?"

The woman—stilled—was lost in some earlier, unkind time. "That is the long story," she finally said. "It is a story of the futility of love, of how you can care so deeply about another that you would gladly sacrifice yourself for them, in any capacity, but how, in the end, it doesn't matter. The body betrays you. Art betrays you. And love, that desperate, flailing thing, betrays almost by definition. Love is the most powerful and the most powerless thing in existence. I am saying that now, but I am sure it has been said before."

"Did you ask for a second opinion?"

"After Bennett was dead?" Olivia shrugged, and her features arranged themselves into a sad, composed smile. "What does an explanation matter when you have lost your child? I had my own. Bennett's commitment to his art had killed him. He had been gassed."

"Gassed?"

"In the Great War."

Paul felt her sadness, her strange resignation. The long story had explained nothing, but she didn't expect him to understand. "But why would that make you stay here in this house, with all these sad memories?"

"Memory? What an odd thing that is. Those little pictures of this past that can be so much more alive than the present but are, by definition, dead. I could not leave here because I could not leave my son. I have a small inheritance and with whatever I had put away for retirement, I was able to stay."

He drained the last of his whiskey and set the glass down on the floor beside his chair. His host sat still, her eyes angled up and to the right, with a pursed and pensive smile. She then inhaled deeply, awakening to the present. "And you must be exhausted," she said. "The bed is already made up. There are some magazines in the room, although they're a bit out of date."

* * *

He did not realize that he had left his phone in his coat until he'd already dressed down to his underwear. He wondered if he should bother retrieving it, because the house was cold and putting his pants on again seemed like one action too many on this eventful day. What a strange woman his host was but somehow hard to discount. His girlfriend, now ex, had found him boring, and he entertained a fantasy of renewing their relationship by relating this story, but it seemed collaterally fascinating. And wasn't it his witnessing without ever really participating that had made her leave him in the end? But maybe she had sensed his peril and sent him a text, a text that he was missing as he read the *London Review of Books* from November 2016, a publication he was reading because it was one that she liked to read. Had he been an artist, would he have been more compelling? His work was so rooted in the earth, in available resources and how to best exploit them. He was involved in identifying, quantifying, selling. That seemed honest to him, not washed in the murkiness of whatever art purported to be, of whatever had filled Bennett's lungs with fluid and condemned the woman to haunt—as what else did one call it?—this house on the moors. He pulled on his pants and padded in bare feet to the door. The house was still, dark, although with a dull illumination creating a soft glow somewhere downstairs, as if a screen were lit up or perhaps the moon had broken through the mist.

He was passing by the hall mirror when a dark oval of shadow shifted suddenly, and he saw it—the figure. There had been something in the mirror that moved, but on closer inspection, he saw that it was just his reflection, altered by light and by his own state of mind that had slowly been assaulted by the woman's deranged storytelling. He continued down the hall to the hooks and began to feel through the coats hanging there for the telltale crackling fabric of his jacket. Then he heard a voice. It was the woman speaking softly upstairs. He stilled himself and listened. She said, "It's only for one night, until the mist lifts." He froze. She must have been speaking to herself. There was a moment's silence, and he renewed his search for the phone, quickly now. He was alarmed by the sound of someone walking in the corridor above, and then hesitant, quiet footsteps sounded on the stairs. He fished around the pockets quickly and found his phone. He felt strangely apologetic for being out of bed—although why?—and he was thinking of his explanation when he turned to face his host.

There at the end of the hallway was not the woman but a young man, unbearably pale, with a shock of black hair, his lips tight together, his eyes dark and wild. The young man stood and eyed him until, through the act of seeing, he seemed to dissolve all matter except for his own. As if time had stopped or folded in upon itself, Paul regarded the figure, who seemed contained in his own thoughts, until he felt himself to be the apparition, the person peering into a reality that he did not fully inhabit. The young man looked out—still, unyielding—and then stepped to walk through the wall that separated the hallway from the kitchen.

He had seen the son.

His rushing blood sounded in his ears. He had watched the figure disappear into some other room that was the kitchen but surely a space less mundane, and from that location he heard a coughing—rasping at first but then blossoming into something liquid—a hacking that would not quit. He felt incapable of movement, but when that ability returned, what would he do? His boots were right there. He could put them on, grab the coat, and head into the fog. Or he could quickly return to his room and spend the night, lights on, watching the door. The story was growing longer and longer still, and the end was not yet in sight.

Muckross Abbey

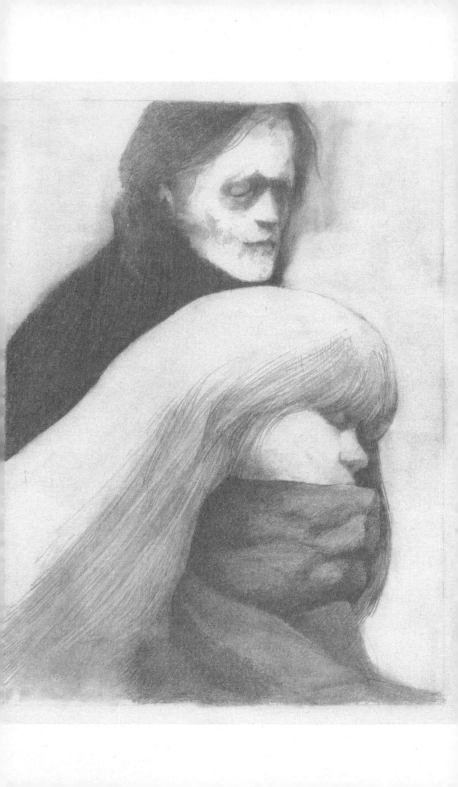

W hat help was needed was not clear. Simone's mother had called me and then quickly handed the phone to her husband, Eric, because she was rapidly becoming inarticulate.

"They can't find her," Eric said. "She's probably all right. You know Simone. She's got a mind of her own." He wasn't very convincing. "Dean is losing it."

I hardly knew Dean. "And the police are involved?"

"Yes. They've started an official search."

"They'll probably find her soon." Dismissive seemed appropriate. "Where in Kerry were they?"

There was some rapid consulting, and I heard papers being moved around. "Muckross? Is that a city?"

"I'll find it. Send me Dean's contact info." I had the phone on speaker and was scanning through flights. "If I leave right now, I can make the four o'clock from Heathrow." And the parents would show up the following day, at which point, we agreed, everything would likely be resolved. I noted the name of the hotel where Dean and Simone had been staying and assured them everything would be all right, because that's what one did in situations like this, although such statements are unfounded and meaningless.

I quickly explained to my assistant what the situation was and she responded with appropriate concern. The office was just a few blocks from my apartment in Bloomsbury and the tube a straight shot to the airport. My bag was still mostly packed from the wedding, which had been in Chicago the week before. If I didn't dawdle, I would be in Shannon by five thirty.

Why had I agreed to go? I blamed the conversation with Simone's parents at the wedding reception, a conversation that we were having because I didn't know any of Simone's friends and wasn't sure what to do with myself. I had talked about my life in London, the glamorous work of agenting, which I allowed to seem as glamorous as they wanted it to be because it would have been ungenerous to set them straight.

Simone and I had been roommates in college. I was the overachieving one, the A student, the grind, and I felt myself hoping—as her parents hoped—that all the work had paid off. I hadn't married, and I suspected they thought it was because I was no fun. But Simone was only marrying now, and we were both nearing forty. As college chums, we'd been close. We had little to fight about. She was typical of her sort of girl—blond, smart enough, athletic—and I was fine with all of that. She referred to me as a Goth, but I stayed indoors because I had too much work to do otherwise and wore black because I was poor and cheap black clothes looked the most like their expensive counterparts. We still saw each other every few years, a dinner together when I had to meet a client in Boston or a weekend in New York if I had a couple of nights in a swanky hotel paid for, a phone call every six months or so. On closer examination, she was probably one of my best friends, although I doubt I would have made the cut for her. For Simone, I was a historical friend, one that was occasionally dusted off to anchor the past to a shifting present that was somehow less real. I had known her when she was "college Simone" and when Simone was with me, she was reacquainted with this younger, successful outing of self. Of the two of us, I had aged better, but this was just the result of my looking remarkably old in my late teens and early twenties. I would probably go to the grave looking like this, and when people told me "you haven't changed a bit" it was usually with mild, justified horror.

I landed in Shannon and picked up the rental car. Southern England was in the grip of a heat wave, but in Ireland the weather was pleasantly dreary. A soft rain was pattering from a gray sky, and the windshield whumped in time with my heartbeat. I followed the GPS to Ballyseede Castle, the hotel in Tralee that I had been instructed to book, where Dean and Simone were staying. Much of my drive was occupied with a phone call to one of my playwrights, who was very upset that his play had received such negative reviews. I, too, was upset but not surprised, as it was a bad play and poorly directed, with the actors afflicted with long pauses as if summoning the strength to deliver the next line. I wasn't sure what he wanted from me as his agent, but I assured him that the play would do better in America, although I found it unlikely that the production would make it out of England. I managed to get him off the phone with the usual line: Henry James, too, had suffered bad reviews and when an unthinking public delivered such a blow, one should take it as a badge of honor. I hoped that my playwrights did not speak among themselves.

As I pulled into the long drive, shaded by ancient trees carpeted in moss, I found myself wondering not only why Simone had disappeared but also why she had married Dean in the first place. They had dated for close to a decade, achieving what seemed an easy stasis, something that marriage could only disturb. But what did I know? I had never been married, and Ashwin, my companion of the last five years, was as hesitant to marry as I was. At least he had the excuse of having been divorced. I didn't like involving myself in things, marriage included, which made me wonder why I had been so easily persuaded to come to Ireland. But I did want to know what had happened to Simone. The only explanation that presented itself was that she had come to her senses and, regretting the marriage, had run off to reassess the situation. Maybe she'd realized that she didn't love him.

Simone had always presented Dean as a completely viable partner. He was even-tempered. He made money. He was blandly handsome. He cooked an inoffensive cassoulet. He checked all the right boxes, and if Dean were something like a car rather than a husband, he would have been a good choice. But Simone had not been passionate about him, as she had not been passionate about her college boyfriends, who had all seemed to be Dean in the making, the exception being Wilkins, whom Simone had dated our sophomore year. Wilkins was an heir to a dynastic family who had made their money in oatmeal, and Simone had been passionate about him. Or maybe she had just been animated by being in the orbit of his obvious derangement. Wilkins had been excitable.

Ballyseede Castle rose in a solid rectangle of well-structured granite. There was a pair of Irish wolfhounds circling idly in the drive and a group of tourists in hiking garb—likely Americans rediscovering their roots—gathered by the door. I parked and took my bag up the front steps and into the reception area. At a small desk dwarfed by a monumental floral arrangement—all lilies and cascading ivy—a woman was working very hard at shuffling inconsequential papers in an effort to ignore my presence.

"Excuse me," I said. "I have a room booked."

She looked up, peering over the rim of her glasses, feigning surprise. "Welcome to Ballyseede Castle," she said.

"Thank you very much."

"And your name?"

"Kelly Chang."

"Oh," she said, suddenly solicitous. "I have a message for you."

The message was from Dean. He said to text as soon as I arrived but not to call as he was trying to stay off his phone in case Simone tried to contact him. He was at Muckross

Abbey with the police. While I was reading the message, a young man had attached himself to my bag, which I clearly did not need help with, having carted it up the steps with little effort. But it was pointless at this stage to argue and as we ascended a small set of steps, crossed a room that seemed permanently set for weddings—a kitsch Haversham nightmare of silk flowers, towering candelabras, and shiny drapes—I was at least pleased for the help to find my room. I followed him down a long corridor, his shoes silent on the carpet, the wheels of my suitcase squeaking gently. I was staying in the new extension and although attempts had been made to bring the annex in line with the rest of the building, robbed of the hunting photos, deer heads, carved wooden dressers, I could have been in a Radisson.

He unlocked the door and wheeled in the suitcase, making a big show of pulling aside the drapes to reveal a good view of the parking lot. He smiled shyly.

The smile got me and I found a five-euro bill. "Is this place haunted?" I asked.

"Yeah, but not this part. Just the old bit. She's supposed to be friendly, but she'll give you a fright."

"Jilted at the altar?"

"How did you know?"

"They usually are."

Google Maps informed me that it was forty-minute drive to Muckross. I texted Dean to tell him I was on my way, but as I was readying to go, Dean texted that he was headed back. I figured the police wanted him out of their hair. I headed for the bar.

The bar area was small and, at that time, empty but for one man sitting sheltered at a corner table scrolling through his phone. From the clatter and burble coming from the dining area, I figured most people were eating. I took a seat at the bar, waiting for the bartender to show up. More photos of Ballyseede's ancestral family were hanging on the walls, women sitting on picnic blankets with their ankles crossed, raising a glass, men shouldering rifles, flanked between dogs and boys holding bunches of drooping, dead rabbits. The gloom of the place was charming. It was a relentless reminder that we are dead for so long and alive so briefly, that life is the anomaly, a brief photo op, something worth attention. The bartender walked in and, bracing himself against the bar, asked, "What can I get you?"

"Can you make a negroni?"

"Sorry, but no. We have no Campari. I'd say we'd just run out, but I don't think we ever had it." He was defeated in that appealing Irish way.

"Then red wine. A cabernet?"

"That I can do."

He poured a good glass, paused, then topped it up, smiling. "Here to see the sights?"

"Not really," I said.

"No?"

"Have you heard about the woman who's gone missing at Muckross Abbey?"

"Oh, yeah. Friend of yours?"

"Yes. I think I am here to babysit her husband."

"She hasn't been gone that long," said the bartender. "I hope they find her soon."

This brief exchange stirred the bar's other patron. He was speedily up from his table and made it to my side in three quick steps. Pulling out the neighboring stool, he asked, "Do you mind if I sit here?" He didn't wait for an answer and settled into the seat. He flexed his hands a couple of times, then extending the right said, "I'm Detective Kettle. So you're a friend of Simone Beekman?"

I looked at his hand. "Beekman? You mean Stein." The hand was still there, so I squeezed it quickly.

"Beekman is her married name."

"Of course," I said. "Yes, I am her friend."

"I'd like to ask you some questions, if that's all right?"

"It is all right, if you don't mind answering some yourself. What happened? I had a brief conversation with Simone's parents, but they weren't exactly articulate."

"And your name is?"

"Kelly Chang."

The detective took a notepad out of his pocket and considered using it but set it on the bar. "So Simone and Dean went to Muckross House and took the last tour. When the tour was finished, Dean had a business call he had to take, so he sat in his car in the car park and Simone walked out to the abbey to take a look. The abbey's about a mile from the house, not far. Dean was supposed to follow after his call was done, but the client kept him on the phone for an hour. It was still bright out when he went to join her, but she was gone. He went back to Muckross House, which was shutting down for the day, but no one had seen her. He wandered around for another hour, tried to call her repeatedly, but she'd disappeared. A family saw her at the abbey at around six p.m., and they were the last to see her."

"Maybe she took a taxi?"

"All of that's been checked. No one saw her walking on the road. There are some regular dog walkers on the grounds and a couple saw her going to the abbey, but that's all." The detective looked at the glass of soda water that the bartender had just set for him. "They're dragging the lake."

"Oh, Jesus," I said. "They think she fell into the lake?"

"Or something similar. We don't know."

"She wouldn't kill herself, if that's what you're implying."

The detective nodded affably and then fixed his eyes on me with intent. "What can you tell me about Dean?"

I considered. "He's a bit dull."

"Were they happy?"

"What? Was it a happy marriage? They'd been married for less than a week." I was getting prickly because the fact

37

that something might actually be wrong had finally set in. The detective's eyes tracked my face, understanding the metric of my thoughts. "I don't know why she'd run off. It seems out of character. And as for Dean, you can take him off your list of suspects. He's incapable of violence. He's docile to a fault. Even their arguments were dull."

"So they argued?"

Where had I dredged up this volatile piece of information? And then I remembered. On one of our weekends in New York, Simone had said that Dean was not a big fan of fun. He didn't understand relaxation. He was happiest when he was working. Simone liked to go to the movies, and Dean didn't understand why they couldn't stay at home and watch Netflix. He'd gone to the movies with her because she wanted to go, but he hadn't really enjoyed it. And, provokingly, he hadn't understood why his acquiescing had failed to solve the problem. Simone enjoyed it, and wasn't that enough? He couldn't make himself enjoy going to the movies. To make it worse, the fight had happened after seeing the Tolkien biopic, which was really boring, making Simone's position difficult to defend. And this had made her angrier. Did the detective want to hear this?

"Are you married?" I asked. I took the silence to mean that he was. "If I were you, I would take Dean off the list of suspects."

"That leaves a very short list."

"How short?"

I was again met with silence.

"I have no reason to defend Dean," I said. "I just want to find out what happened to Simone, and I think looking at Dean is a waste of time."

"You could be right there," said the detective. "He was on the phone with the client for that full hour and after that mostly accompanied by people who were trying to help him find her. But maybe something happened to Simone before the call."

I ordered a sandwich at the bar and the detective did too. He asked me about the history of their relationship, what Dean did to make his money, if I'd noticed anything at the wedding. I'm sure he—or some other detective—had already asked Dean all these questions, but the man was doing his job and if I hadn't been sitting there helping him do it, I don't know how else I'd have occupied the time.

Dean arrived a short while later. I could hear his anxious voice as he tried to rid himself of the suddenly solicitous receptionist, and I rose, with the detective, to meet him in the vestibule.

"Dean," I said to interrupt.

"Kelly. Thank God you're here."

He rushed over but as we'd never hugged before, stopped just short of me. I opened my arms in a moment of generosity and he collapsed against me. Whatever strength had been holding him together deserted, and he began sobbing. I looked over his shoulder at the detective who understood what my expression—which communicated that I'd told him as much—implied. The detective made a few courteous comments about how the whole police force was mobilized and would be working through the night, that Dean should get some rest because it would be best for all if he were alert and capable the next day, and then he left out the front door. I led Dean back into the bar where my third glass of cabernet was waiting for me. I ordered Dean a whiskey, which he looked at wondering if he should partake, and then he grabbed the glass and took a slug. The bartender, being skilled, gave us a wide berth and began busying himself at the other end of the bar.

"I thought everything was fine," Dean said. "The whole tour she was smiling at me as we wandered around Muckross House. She was asking questions. She knew I had to take the call. She had made peace with it. One of the reasons we're in Ireland is that I could write it off if I stopped by the Dublin office, so she knew I'd have to do some work. She was happy to see the abbey by herself. She wanted the quick walk because we'd been eating so much heavy food."

That sounded like Simone. "How was Dublin?"

Dean shrugged. "We were staying at a hotel in Temple Bar. It was a bit noisy at night but walking distance to everything."

"That's not what I mean, Dean. How were things with you and Simone?"

His voice dropped to a whisper and he eyed the bartender as he carried a crate of glasses out of the room. "We got into an argument," he said.

"What about?"

"About Joyce."

"Who's Joyce?" I thought it had to be an ex.

"James Joyce, the writer. Simone was always telling me that I didn't understand art, which I don't, but she thought it would be fun if we read *Dubliners* together while we were in Dublin, and so we'd have something to talk about at dinner." Dean was still confused by this proposal. "But I had a deadline, so when I was supposed to be reading the book, I was actually finishing up a report." He shook his head. "The only story I know at all is 'The Dead.' I had to read it in high school. I could only remember bits and pieces, you know, the girl taking Gabriel's coat and saying 'palaver' and then the snow being 'general' and something about a guy who used to throw rocks at the window."

"Michael Furey," I said.

"Yes, him. At any rate, Simone knew I hadn't read the book. She totally overreacted. She said I knew nothing about passion and that I was a philistine." Dean shot me a bewildered look. "I think she was having second thoughts about the marriage, but a lot of people do that and work their way through it. So I just let her go on. And she said that she had a Michael Furey of her own, someone who loved her passionately, and that she broke his heart. She was sobbing. I had no idea what she was going on about."

"What did you do?"

"I poured her a glass of wine. What else could I do?"

"Do you think any of this is connected to Simone's disappearance?"

Dean swept the bar with another nervous look. We were alone. "I don't know how," he said. "But other than that, she seemed fine. Do you know anything about this guy?"

"Simone's Michael Furey?" I knew she had to have been talking about Wilkins. The breakup had been bad. Simone had committed to spending a semester in Spain before the two had gotten together. Even though Simone hadn't wanted to leave him, she felt it would have been ridiculous not to go. Wilkins was absurdly upset, which I told her was a warning sign. Simone had gone to Spain. Once there, she had found herself suddenly enamored of a Spaniard named Alva. She and Alva frequented nightclubs where, in true American fashion, Simone was often flamboyantly drunk, having never been able to drink in public before. In an unfortunate turn, Simone had found herself pregnant. This all happened in the first half of the semester. Someone had shown her how to make free calls by triggering the pay-phone hang up switch and she would call me at night, increasingly desperate. She needed money for an abortion. She had pawned a pair of gold earrings but was still four hundred dollars short. Could

I loan her the money? As I was poor, I also saved and sent her the necessary funds. As she was rich, I knew that she would pay me back. It was an intense couple of weeks, but the resolution seemed peaceful enough, until she returned to school—and to Wilkins—who had been kept in the dark the whole time.

"She might have been talking about a guy named Wilkins, done with long ago," I said. Truth is, Simone had been in love with Wilkins. As soon as she returned from Spain, she got back together with him and in the grip of poorly thought through honesty, told him about Alva. Wilkins forgave her but now saw that he had the upper hand in the relationship and was so stifling and controlling that it made Simone's life impossible. I wasn't sure how they finally broke up. I remembered him howling outside our dorm window and security taking him away. And then a couple of years later, he was dead. "I have a hard time see-ing how Simone's college boyfriend fits in with any of this. Anyway, Wilkins is dead. I think he committed suicide, but it was a while after they'd broken up."

"If we're talking about the same guy, I don't think he did kill himself," Dean said. "He got some fast-acting cancer. Near the end, Simone went to visit him, and he made her promise never to get married."

"Really?"

"Yeah. It was just some weird college thing." A thing that, given Dean's expression, was gaining new importance.

"Well," I said. "Simone never mentioned it to me." But she wouldn't have, would she? Why would she tell judgmental Kelly, who had loaned her the money for the abortion, who would graduate with high honors, who had always thought Wilkins annoying, who had never—and might never be—in love? Our friendship had its limits and my sympathy was a practical thing: good for emergency loans, bad for listening to the excesses of incontinent emotion. Simone had known and respected that.

Dean and I left the bar before midnight. I thought I'd have a hard time falling asleep, but the damp pillow on my cheek was the last thing I remembered until a gentle yet insistent knocking woke me up. Was there knocking? Yes. Someone was at the door. I checked my phone. It was 5:00 a.m. I cracked the door without slipping the chain. It was Dean. He was wearing a pair of Wellingtons and a bulky sweater.

"Did you sleep at all?" I said.

He nodded. "Will you come with me to Muckross?"

"Now?"

"What if she's out there in a ditch or if there's a clue that we'll miss? There's supposed to be heavy rain later in the morning."

I thought it best if I drive. Dean, apparently good with directions, had no need of the GPS, and our journey was mostly silent. We picked up coffee and sandwiches at a convenience store along the way. Dean was scrolling through his phone that was hooked up to charge on the car's console to keep the battery at full power.

"What are you looking at?" I asked.

"Just trying to keep busy I guess. I'm reading about Muckross House and the abbey, seeing if anything strange has happened there before."

"Has there?"

"Things were pretty bad for the Catholics under Cromwell," said Dean. "And there's a legend of the Brown Man. His newlywed bride discovered him at Muckross Abbey eating a corpse." Dean set down the phone. "Maybe there's some weirdo hanging around the abbey."

"The Brown Man? Seriously?" I questioned, but my voice did not have the bite it might have because we were clutching at straws. At the gates of the property, we were questioned and allowed in. I suppose they thought it was Dean's right to search along with the police, although it was hard to figure out what we could do that sniffer dogs and divers and systematic searching could not do better. But maybe it was good that we were there. While I was trying to formulate a course of action, a policewoman came over and asked Dean if he could please identify something. A scarf had been found. I saw the scarf in the policewoman's hands—purple, hand knit. And yes, it was Simone's scarf, but what it established who could know? It was accepted fact that Simone had been walking around in that area and the scarf seemed to say nothing but that she had been walking around in that area. I left Dean to the police and decided to follow the signs to the abbey because there was something about it that had to be significant. If I were a less logical person, I would have felt that the building was calling me to it, because even without the signs I was strangely able to find my way. I seemed to know the general direction across the fields and anticipated every necessary turn. There was something familiar in the carriageways shaded with vaulting tree limbs, dotted with horse dung. Branches rattled by birds and a stiff wind bending the higher limbs of the trees were matched in a music of urgency.

The abbey revealed itself as if slowly focusing into reality from a nineteenth-century watercolor. The ruined roof and crumbling walls seemed to anchor the building solidly in a past rather than record the march of time. I could hear a conversation happening on the other side of the fortification. When I rounded the corner, I saw three police officers—two young men and an older woman—sitting on a low wall. An ancient yew grew in the courtyard fronting the building.

"Hello," said a young officer when he saw me. "Miss, I'm not sure you should be here."

"I'm Kelly Chang. I'm a friend of Simone Stein. I mean Beekman. I'm a friend of Simone Beekman. They let me in." I gestured over my shoulder.

"Right," said the young man. He inhaled deeply and thought things through. "Well maybe it's good that you have a look. You might see something that we've missed, although the dogs have been through here already. And forensics picking up prints and such."

"Did they find anything?"

"They did find her scarf. A lot of people come through here this time of year, so we're not sure what the prints will yield. But they're questioning everyone."

"Have a look around," said the woman. "You're her friend. Maybe you'll have some insight."

I wanted to confess then that I had not been that close to Simone, but being unsure what that would achieve, I simply nodded.

"Avoid touching the surfaces," the woman added. "And any little thing that comes to you might help."

The graves were crowded on the uneven ground. Some looked to be quite recent, and one had flowers that were now wilted but might have been fresh a week before. A profound silence settled all around me, although through it I could still hear the patter of voices, the somber tones of the police understanding the gravity of the situation, still handing around the well-worn facts.

I could have sworn right then that someone said my name, sighing it, in the wind that was causing a branch to brush against the rough wall of the abbey. The birds were suddenly quiet. The sky was turning from a cold blue to a

bruised purple. Rain was imminent I thought or just a deep-
ening damp. I felt an ache inside my chest and then a flood-
ing sorrow. I knew that if I could bring myself to leave the
abbey, the pain would leave me, but I felt compelled to keep
going, to enter into the dark hall. Why was I so suddenly
affected? I felt burdened by a great grief, but it was not a grief
that I had ever known. I took another step and then was
returned to a memory, to the night that Wilkins was calling
up to Simone from outside our dorm room, when security
had dragged him away. At the time, I thought that Simone
was in love with the drama of Wilkins's performance. I'd
been incapable of comforting her, not put off by her flood
of emotion nor suspicious but instead just indifferent—too
sensible to attend to it. I continued through the abbey,
drawn to a set of stone stairs. Wilkins. This all had to do
with Wilkins. I remembered walking through the Whit-
ney with Simone, her stopping by a Hopper painting—*Soir
Bleu*—and saying, "Wilkins was terrified of clowns," and my
inadequate response that Wilkins seemed to be terrified of
everything. I remembered, as my footsteps sounded on the
flagstones, that she had managed to bring up that long-ago
relationship with me every time we met, once a reference
to a poem—atrocious—that he had written for her, once
the way his hair fell across his eyes. And in every mention
of him, I had dismissed the thought as frivolous, as the sort
of girlhood memories that someone like Simone—stuck in
a dull present—would try to animate in order to animate

herself. And once she had said—this thought came to me as I made the first of a set of stone stairs—that I was the only friend she still had who'd known Wilkins, who had met him. I had often wondered why Simone bothered to keep up with me, her college chum, who was proudly no fun and with whom she had nothing in common, and I realized it was not for me but for Wilkins. I was there to remind her that Wilkins had really happened. I was now in the middle of the staircase, and the weight of emotion was becoming unbearable. I thought of Simone's desperation at seeing Dean across the tables of her life, hearing his breathing as he slept beside her on a series of beds, and how she must have married him because her fear of this future could only be dispensed with by entering into the very thing that frightened her. How I knew this I can't adequately explain, but it was as if Simone had descended upon me. I felt her mind clutching at ways to make her honeymoon bearable, her presentation to Dean of *Dubliners* and then a memory that *Dubliners* had been gifted to Simone by Wilkins. He'd believed that when he and Simone read the same book, that as they were looking at the same pages, they were in each other's minds. He could not bear that there should be a part of her that was not his or a part of his that she did not own. All of this had seemed so overly dramatic, so indulgent, so silly. And as I did my college work late into the night, Simone was rolling in her bed unable to sleep, I thought because I had the light on, but in truth because she was suffering and she could find no way out of her love for Wilkins. Or was he already dead, a death that she had chosen not to share with me in case I made light of it? I was now at the head of the stairs and the chill of it had made me start to shiver, although the temperature could not have justified that. Shaking to the very heart of my bones, I brought myself to the small window. I now felt a dread along with a breaking heart that was not my heart but that I felt as keenly. I braced myself against the ledge and feeling a dizzying cold still the air, allowed myself to look.

She stood on the ground below me, her eyes fixed with a knowing calm. Her hair was not moved by the wind, despite the fact that it was loose. She was luminously pale. Through my demented state, a flicker of reason told me to call out. Simone had been found, but I knew that somehow my eyes were telling me something quite different. Besides, she was wearing the purple scarf, the one the police had shown to me. Still, I wanted to shout, if for nothing but to wake myself from this feeling of derangement, but Simone raised her finger to her lips, ordering me to silence. And then, as if she had never been there, my eyes presented me the sight of an open field and wind battering leaves and the birdsong that in the aftermath of unreal silence seemed deafening. I was returned to myself. I was no longer shivering and I ran.

"Is everything all right?" asked the policewoman, rising as I rushed from the graveyard. "You look like you've seen a ghost."

"No," I said, adding a vague, "I'm just a little dizzy."

"Poor thing. We'll find your friend. Don't you worry."

"Do you want some coffee?" said one of the young men. He had a thermos. He poured a cup and extended it to me. "Sorry I've only got the one cup."

I took the coffee and drank it, nodding my thanks. It struck me as an act of extreme kindness, although I knew it was just a simple gesture, the sort of thing done by a person with good manners and an easy way with others. Simple, alien things.

As I approached Muckross House I saw that Simone's parents had arrived. There was still a great deal of activity, a sense of purpose underscored by the crackling of radios. The dogs strained against their leashes, their kind eyes tracing over their handlers; in the distance other dogs were moving quickly, their noses lowered as they zigzagged across the grass. A diver in a wet suit was smoking a cigarette. Simone's father had seen me, so I had to make my greeting. I wandered over, wondering when they would learn that Simone was dead.

"We all need to stay positive," said Simone's father. "For Simone," he added.

Dean was making purposeful strides toward us, his face lit up with optimism. "Kelly," he said. "They found her phone."

Somehow I found myself in a tight huddle of people looking at the small screen. The last text was one to Dean saying that Simone had reached the abbey.

"Check the photos," said someone. I was in a daze and not paying close attention to who said what but cast my eyes in the same direction as everyone else. There was a selfie of Simone mugging for the camera like a Brontë heroine, the graves behind her. And then another, no doubt taken to be edited to sepia and posted on Instagram.

"That's not the last picture taken, is it?"

"No."

In the next shot a figure could be seen in the corner—almost cropped out and strangely out of focus—a dark pillar of person with no discernible features.

"Keep going."

In the next picture, the figure was closer. Simone was still smiling out, unaware. In the next, it was obviously a young man with dark hair falling across his brow. And in the next he was closer, and his expression was filled with such intent as to seem almost malevolent.

"Who is he?" asked Dean as the picture was expanded to show a face that I alone knew, the face of a man who had been dead for twenty years.

I stepped away from the group and went to the diver, asking him for a cigarette, which he quickly gave to me. I smoked it listening to the police as they ordered their tasks:

make copies, distribute, ask if anyone has seen a man fitting this description—dark hair, white, in his twenties.

"I guess that's a break in the case," said the diver.

And I nodded, although I knew that by drawing closer to the truth, we had stepped further from the possibility of any understanding.

The Dead Children

"Dead, quite dead," said Tom. "Slumped over his desk—a face-plant into a book."

"You said it was his heart?" she asked.

"Yes. A massive coronary. Surprised everyone."

"That is very sad," said Judith. She hadn't known Anton Galchek well, but anyone's death was sobering.

Judith nodded to Tom, signaling an end to the conversation, although that seemed an elevated term for their exchange. It was a Friday, 5:00 p.m., and already dark. The department meeting had been mercifully short and other faculty members lingered, chatting on the library steps as if the half hour handed back to them needed to be immediately squandered. Some of the younger instructors would, no doubt, be heading for a drink at one of the local bars, but they wouldn't ask her to join. And she wouldn't go anyway. There was a detective show that she was slowly working through on Netflix that was calling to her, but perhaps she'd stop by her office and finish the last three papers that needed grading. Then tomorrow would be free and she could use the time to get a jump on her paper, a fluff piece on servants—Mrs. Danvers from *Rebecca* and Mrs. Grose from *The Turn of the Screw*—that she was presenting at an on-campus symposium the following semester. Also, Judith was not quite ready to go home. She crossed the quad to Carew Hall, noting the drop in temperature. Somewhere, a wood fire was burning and the scent of it tinged the air. A smell like that could use a glass of red wine she thought. Judith had just fished her ID out of her wallet and was touching it to the security pad to let her into the building when she heard the woman call out.

"Judie," came the woman's voice. "Judie Denlow."

Judith turned, alarmed by two intimacies: the first, her name shortened to Judie, the second, the Australian accent. The woman was standing half-lit in the streaming lamplight. She was wearing a knee-length floral dress, a coat of hard tweed, and sensible shoes. A sensible black handbag hung on her shoulder.

"Do we know each other?" Judith asked.

"We did," she said.

The woman must have been near seventy. And there was something familiar about her, which Judith found unsettling. "How can I help you?"

"I'm not sure you can," said the woman. "And it has been a long time, but you two were so close. She'd be your age now, although I don't think she'd be a professor. You were always the more clever of the two. The cleverest girl in the school. Everyone thought so."

But not pretty, not nice. She did know this woman, although it had been forty years since she'd seen her. Judith was flooded with cold, unforgiving adrenaline. "Mrs. Begley, am I right?" said Judith.

"That's right," said the woman, but she made no move to come closer, just stood washed by light, her bare face raised with an accusing vulnerability.

"What brings you to Vermont?"

"I wanted to see the sights," said Mrs. Begley.

"And is the college one of them?" Judith forced a smile.

"No. Actually, I just wanted to see you." The woman held her eyes, unblinking.

Perhaps a cup of tea would do it. Just some tea, a little reminiscence of her childhood in Perth, and then the woman would be on her way. But where? The two restaurants that doubled as coffee shops and bars would no doubt be bustling because of the meeting, and Judith had no desire to be sitting with this odd relic of her childhood under the watchful gaze of her colleagues.

"Where are you staying?" asked Judith. "Are you at the hotel?"

"Yes. It's very nice," said Mrs. Begley.

"Perhaps I could make us some tea at home and then drop you after? I do have some grading, but it would be a shame not to catch up, if only for an hour."

"That's very kind of you," said the woman. But her eyes had narrowed when Judith indicated that their proceedings would be finite, that she had an hour but no longer. And Judith's need to control things—a carryover from childhood—was no more popular with Mrs. Begley than it had been forty years earlier.

Judith's house was a low-slung split-level on a side street two blocks from the college. From the outside, it was plain verging on ugly, particularly in the winter and early spring. In a few months, the garden would make all forgivable, a slow performance that kicked off with drunken, nodding peonies and dilating poppies, followed by a swarm of rose and honeysuckle and clematis and sweet pea. The humming-birds would hover and battle, while bees groped shivering flowers. But now, as Judith led Mrs. Begley up the poorly shoveled walkway, all there was to see was a frozen dog turd that had sunk into the snow of its own initial heat. Tatters, the donor of the yard's sole decoration, was now scrabbling and howling at the window of the neighbor's house. When Judith raised her head and leveled a look at the dog, he dropped from view, silenced.

"No pets of your own?" asked Mrs. Begley.

"No. I don't much like animals, and the feeling seems to be mutual."

"Emma loved animals. Dogs and cats and guinea pigs."

"I remember her having a canary."

"And the fish. She cleaned the tank every week and when one of the fish died, she wouldn't let us flush it. She said it was undignified. She buried it in the garden and made a little cross for it out of icy pole sticks."

One hour, thought Judith as the key turned in the lock. Perhaps there was nothing here to fear but tedium.

"Emma would have loved to have a cat or a dog."

"I remember Mr. Begley being allergic."

"No, no pets for Stan, although he did love the horses."

Judith remembered that too. Mr. Begley on a Sunday afternoon, planted in front of the television, watching race after race. All the races looked the same. One horse would have to win, and that was grand. But one horse would have to lose, and that—no matter how unavoidable—was always upsetting to Emma. She would want to know the horse's name—but only the one that came in last—and would fret. Mr. Begley would say, "Better luck next time." Every time.

Mrs. Begley followed Judith into the kitchen. "I have a lovely Moroccan mint or some rooibos perhaps?"

"Lipton is fine for me," said Mrs. Begley.

Judith did not have Lipton but rather an expensive black tea blend. The gas burner ticked then blew to life, and Judith set the kettle with a clang.

"Lovely kitchen," said Mrs. Begley. Was Judith detecting approbation in the woman's tone?

"I've lived in this house for fifteen years, which has given me time to get it right."

"Alone all that time?"

"Not all of it." Judith made a show of using the little cast iron teapot and set it down at the kitchen table with a tasteful, earthenware cup. "Well," she said. "How is Mr. Begley? And how are you?"

"Mr. Begley is dead. It was unavoidable."

"Unavoidable?"

"Old people die, you see. You mourn them for an appointed time, but they don't take over your life with mourning. You miss them in a good, sensible way. You don't have to shake the feeling that something must have happened, that you didn't deserve the grief, or that your child didn't deserve to die."

"Mrs. Begley, I'm afraid I don't understand. Why are you here?"

"I know you haven't told me everything. I saw you, seated at the back of the church at Emma's funeral. You were alone. And you were giggling, giggling away, hiding it and poorly, behind your hands, behind the hymnal. But your eyes were lit up and I could see. I wanted to go after you, to shake you and make you tell me why she was up there on that building, how she fell, but Stan wouldn't let me. He said you were just a child. How could you know anything? But you did. And now you are no longer a child. You are going to tell me." She poured herself some tea. "Do you have any sugar?"

Judith had been about to sit but stood back from her chair. She wondered how long a taxi would take to arrive but thought driving the woman might be the better option. "Mrs. Begley, I am afraid I'm going to have to ask you to leave."

A door slammed upstairs, not violently but with enough force to startle the guest. Judith followed Mrs. Begley's eyes as they looked beyond the entry of the kitchen to the foot of the stairs. "I will leave after I get my answers. The longer you take to give them, the longer you will have to put up with my company."

Judith considered, then placed the sugar bowl on the table. What was the harm in tossing this woman a few scraps from the past? She pulled the cork from a bottle of Malbec that was on the counter and poured herself a glass. "We were playing a game, that's all," Judith said. She took a seat across from Mrs. Begley, drinking before setting the glass down. "All the kids played at the site. It was easy to get under the wire fence. We'd pulled it up and made a hole. We called it the Tunnel. There was this one place where you jumped from one ledge to another. We all did it. One of us was bound to fall. And then one of us did."

Mrs. Begley nodded to herself. "I know all that," she said.

"Then you know it all," responded Judith.

Mrs. Begley rapped her nails on the table, as if she were controlling anger, and said, "Judie, don't be one of those clever girls who makes the mistake that everyone else is stupid. Emma was terrified of heights. She would never have gone up on that building unless someone made her do it. She couldn't even go up the DNA Tower in Kings Park. She certainly would never have tried to jump from one ledge to another."

"But that's precisely what she did."

"And now you will tell me why."

Judith inhaled deeply and held it. Upstairs, the door that slammed was now creaking slowly open. If she didn't speak soon, Mrs. Begley would be sure to hear the progression of footsteps. And why not tell the old woman what had happened? Perhaps Judith was just holding the secret out of habit. "It was one of the rules of the game that you had to do whatever they said. And we did."

"They?"

"We had wild imaginations and had convinced ourselves, well, it's hard to explain."

"It is easier if one starts at the beginning," said Mrs. Begley, "and doesn't leave anything out."

But where to start? "I suppose it began with hide-and-seek. We weren't allowed to play it, because, as you know, Loreto Nedlands had some dangerous places and the nuns' quarters were forbidden, but we did used to sneak in there." Of the students, only Judith had reason to enter that region of the Old Building because—strangely—the mimeograph machine, housed in a small closet, was situated there, ostensibly to prevent students from recreational inhalation of the chemicals. Judith—being clever—was often done with her work early and called on to do errands, like reeling off copies. She had seen the derelict nuns lying in their beds. One had a long arc of a nose, razor cheekbones, and yellow, impossibly taut skin. Even the nun's eyelids seemed stretched thin. Her mouth was always open and the sound, an even gasping, had always reminded Judith of the ocean. "So, we'd hide in the nuns' quarters. And then after being caught, needed a new place. We tried the Hall." The Hall had a decent-size stage with wings, long windows set high, and row after row of punitive benches that could be moved aside for dance class. "There was nowhere really to hide in there. We'd sort of dodge around the wings, get behind the chests." Once, Judith had gotten trapped in one of the chests and had to scream to be let out. "Emma was not good at hide-and-seek. She'd get too nervous and usually leapt out before she was found. But one time, she had us absolutely stumped. We couldn't find her. We called for her. It was me and Jackie Snow and that girl Hannah, whose mother was Jewish. And Orla. We thought Emma might have left, gone to the bathroom or something. But she came out. She had found a secret space under the stage. One of the panels was apparently a door. She said there was lots of old stuff in there, that it went far, far back. We decided to come back with a torch." Judith got up to get the wine.

"Emma would never have been able to stay alone in the dark for so long, not in such a scary place," said Mrs. Begley. "You said so yourself."

"And that's why I remember it. Emma was smiling to herself and didn't seem frightened at all." The wine gurgled into the glass. "I brought a torch to school the next day."

Mrs. Begley looked at Judith thoughtfully, with a patience that had been sustained over the last four decades.

"Well, there was stuff down there. We'd lived on rumors of tunnels beneath the school and there was a story that when the Japanese started bombing Darwin, escape routes had been dug. We'd looked for the tunnels before in the storeroom by the amphitheater, squeezing through the gap in the doors left by a loose chain." All children were universally thin in those days. "So we thought we might have found a passage. There were old newspapers dating from the forties, broken chairs, primers. But the find was a scrap of lace. Emma found it, picked it out of the dust. She tied it around her wrist. We didn't know why. She said it belonged to someone named Clara."

"Clara? Clara who?"

"We didn't know." The girls were determined to find out. But how? "And I came up with the idea of a Ouija board. A neighbor had one, made by Parker Brothers." This neighbor was older and richer and had many things, all of which she had made available to Judith when she babysat her. "I said that I could make one on paper. It's easy enough. You just write down the letters and numbers and make a place for 'Yes' and 'No' and 'Goodbye.' I did it on a piece of paper using a shot glass to make the circles. I knew the nuns were against that sort of thing, as were my parents, so I kept it hidden. And we tried it out the next day."

Judith remembered sitting on the floor of the art room with the door shut. The bright November light was streaming through the window, and it seemed that in such intense sun nothing scary would really happen. The smell of cheap paint and soap—those great gray bars that streaked and cracked and barely lathered—held in the room. "We sat in a circle on the floor, Orla, Jackie, Hannah, Emma, and I. We put our fingers lightly on the glass and asked for Clara to show herself. Nothing happened at first, and then the glass started moving wildly. Hannah ran out of the room, frightened. Jackie started giggling, so we knew she'd been moving the glass. Orla was giggling too. They thought it was stupid, so they left. Then it was just Emma and me." And Emma would not cheat. Judith knew that. After the other girls were gone, the room had felt oddly still, filled with both promise and dread. Emma had rested one finger lightly on the glass, as had Judith. Slowly, the glass began to move in a gradual arc, hitting first the number one and then, after a pause, moving to number two. "With just me and Emma doing it, we got the number twelve. I asked if it was Clara." The glass moved swiftly then. "The answer was 'Yes.' Then Emma asked if she had died at twelve, and the answer was 'Yes' again."

"But how do you know that Emma wasn't moving the glass? She was an imaginative child. You were too."

"It was possible that we were carried away at first, lying to ourselves. But then Clara directed us to get her notebook. She said it was in the drawer of her desk, in the storage room." Hearts pounding, Emma and Judith had rolled up the paper board and put it and the shot glass at the back of a cupboard behind a crate of cleaning supplies. Nervously they took the broad steps out of the building into daylight and squeezed between the gapping doors of the storage room. The glass indicated that the desk was in the back, remarkable because there was a C and a W scratched into its surface. It took a half hour, nearly all the time left during the lunch break, but they found it after wiping many dusty surfaces with the bottom edges of their pinafores. The desk lid lifted with a groan and there it was, a small blue notebook with a torn cover and the name Clara Watt written on it in stilted cursive. "So we found the notebook. I took it home and read it." Judith could still feel the wonder at holding the notebook in her hands, the pages soft, resistant to opening, held together by dust and time. "It was mostly handwriting exercises, blots of ink, scratches from when the pen was not cooperating. But on one of the pages there was an exchange in pencil, across the top. I suppose it was Clara and another student, writing to each other so they would not be punished for talking." Judith remembered the first line: *You're a baby. You'll never do it.*

"What did it say?"

"It was a dare, just a couple of lines back and forth, about a tree. There was a nest up there and the two girls were seeing who was brave enough to climb to it. Emma and I went back to the Ouija board. We thought that Clara must have fallen and that had killed her, but we got no response. Clara had gone silent." And maybe they should have left it there. It was a good story, ready for slumber parties then and for their children when they grew up. But the mystery did not seem over, and after the thrill of the bit of lace and the notebook and the scrape of glass against paper, aiming for goals at the netball ring no longer appealed.

Judith was not sure how to go forward. She and Emma had consulted the board with no results for several days. And then Judith was tasked with running off a series of programs for the upcoming Sports Day and found herself in the nuns' quarters. She had raced through her maths equations in record time and her classmates would be laboring for at least another half hour before they'd be ready to move on to the next lesson, so Judith was not in a rush. She turned the mimeograph wheel, making sure to inhale as deeply as she could, dizzying herself, then made her way back to the passage that led to the classrooms. But as she passed the door of the ocean-breathing nun, she had an idea. How old was this woman? Maybe she had known Clara.

"There was an old nun, Sister Barry, and I decided to ask her if she'd known a Clara Watt." Judith sat by the old woman's bed, not sure of what to say, then, suddenly inspired, leaned in to the waxlike ear and said, *Sister, will you bless me?* The old nun's eyes shuddered open, and the hand, thin and beautiful with its network of forking veins and gently curving digits, rested on Judith's head. She felt the blessing enter her, a sort of warm sensation. Then the nun removed her hand and, flickering her gaze across Judith's head with curiosity, asked, *Why are you here?* And Judith said, *I have been sent by Clara Watt. Did you know her?* "The nun was deep in dementia, and when I asked her if she knew Clara, she responded that she did. She knew that Clara was dead but spoke of her as if she were alive. We were right about the tree. Clara had fallen, broken her back, and lain on the grass gasping for several minutes before she died. The nun had seen it all. So the mystery should have been done with then, but she said to me, *Jane's the one that did it. You should ask Jane.*" Judith asked where she might find her, find this Jane, and Sister Barry gestured with her graceful, narrow hand. *They are all here, all the dead children. And they will find you.*"

"Jane?" said Mrs. Begley, nudging her on, but Judith had risen from the table, the wine now emptied. She found the whiskey in the cabinet above the microwave and poured herself a good portion.

"We returned to the Ouija board and asked for Jane, and that is when the game really began."

"The game?"

"When Emma and I became the dead children." Jane had instructed, sliding the glass, that they ask again for Clara. And when they did, Emma's eyes started to quiver. She lifted her fingers off the glass and stretched them, cat-like. A strangeness came over her and when her eyes flicked open, she had leveled a look of astonishment at Judith and asked, *Where is Jane?* Judith pulled back from the board, knowing that some wrong thing was happening. *Emma?* The girl before her shuddered, wrinkled her nose in a way that Judith had never seen Emma do before. *Who is Emma? I am Clara.* And then Emma said, in a surprisingly commanding voice, *Put your finger on the glass.* Barely had the glass begun to move when Judith felt a chill come over her and suddenly she was hovering above the room. Below her, she could see herself and Emma sitting at the board and giggling, but the voices sounded strange. That was not her laughter and not Emma's. Emma was nowhere. Judith struggled to find her voice, but she was silent, a shadow, and she watched with horror as she and her friend leaped up from the board, rolled it and stowed it, and then released themselves from the art room and into the warm light outside. "We would call them, Clara and Jane, on the board, and then it was as if we were no longer in our bodies. We were no longer real, just spirits, and had to watch ourselves while we were trapped in some sort of half-life. We would listen in on their conversations." Once, Jane told a story of seeing Sister Barry with a Sister Enda, and Sister Enda's veil was on the floor, and Sister Barry was greedily kissing her, those beautiful hands kneading Sister Enda's cropped black hair. But mostly they ran and played, climbed and sang. When they were out on the playground, the other children avoided them, made nervous by the girls' sudden raucousness or just knowing in that animal way that children have when something is wrong. "It was always a struggle to get them back to the board, but we were alive and that gave us some power." Like children at the end

71

of recess, Jane and Clara would trudge back to the board, and Emma and Judith would regain themselves. It was with some exhaustion.

"But why did you keep doing it?" asked Mrs. Begley. She had grown pale with unquestioning fear, somehow knowing that Judith was speaking the truth.

"Why do people do such things? I suppose we felt special, but I was scared. The game got more and more dangerous." Once, she had watched herself dangling off the second-floor balcony, holding to the top rail. Judith would have not been able to scramble back. But it was Jane, and Jane was strong, a real athlete. She'd watched herself hook her foot back over the edge and pull herself to safety. Jane was domineering, challenging, and Clara always obeyed. "And it was after school one day that Jane and Clara decided to slip under the fence around the new building. Jane must have bullied Clara to the second story." The building was far from complete, just rough concrete floors and pillars, rebar poking out. Other children, too, had sneaked in and the counting from hide-and-seek could be heard echoing off the unfinished walls from somewhere on the ground floor. "Jane wanted Clara to jump from one ledge to a lower ledge, obviously a dangerous thing to do, and when Clara wouldn't do it—"

"My Emma was pushed?"

Judith nodded wearily. She took some whiskey. Mrs. Begley would have to take a taxi home or sleep on the couch in the study.

"You killed her," said Mrs. Begley, an accusation delivered with a wavering voice.

"Oh, no. I loved Emma. It wasn't me, Mrs. Begley. It was Jane."

"This is nonsense. This is ridiculous nonsense. My Emma is dead, and all you can do is tell me this outlandish tale of ghosts and dead children?" She was finding some outrage, but it was tempered with suspicion that Judith was sincere.

"Mrs. Begley, if you don't believe me, you can ask her yourself."

"Ask who?"

"Emma. You can ask Emma." Judith ground the chair legs across the floor, rising clumsily from the table. She went to the sideboard and pulled out the top drawer. Reaching around the back, behind the neatly folded tablecloths and linen napkins, she found the object, which responded to her grasp with an incriminating crumple of paper. The shot glass, too, was in there, clouded with age and emblazoned with—of all things—a cartoon sandgroper, with Mickey Mouse eyes and cheerful yellow wings that had been popular in Perth in the late seventies. Judith sat back down and unrolled the paper. The circles had faded, the paper yellowed, but the letters and numbers were still clear. Judith set the teacup on one corner, the empty wine bottle on another and managed to get the paper flat with her glass and a coaster. "Put your finger on the glass," Judith instructed.

"My finger?"

"Just lightly. Float it there. You'll see."

At first the glass did not move, but slowly it shuddered from its spot and began the first of a series of slow circles. The glass came to rest at the E, then the M, dodged briefly aside before returning, and then swerved to the A. The cabinet doors began to rattle and the chiming of disturbed crystal could be heard. The light dimmed briefly, then returned to its strength. Mrs. Begley watched her trembling finger on the glass, watched it move to 1, dodging before returning. It paused there for moment. That unseen upstairs door shut with sudden force. Mrs. Begley looked up to see Judie's eyes half open, the whites visible and the pupils quivering upward. The glass moved speedily through the "Goodbye" at the bottom of the board and came to rest.

Judie opened her eyes suddenly. She broke into a smile, the first that Mrs. Begley had seen. "Mummy?" came the voice. What kind of trick was this?

"Who are you?"

"Mummy, what's wrong? Aren't you happy to see me? It's been such a long time, and your hair . . ."

"My hair?"

"It's all gray. I tried to come home, but I couldn't. It's the board. And I have to stay with Judie, you see. Is Daddy really dead?"

"Why are you doing this?" Mrs. Begley said. "Stop it. It isn't funny, and it isn't clever."

"Stop what? It's sad that Daddy's dead. But we can get a dog now? And name it—"

"And name it what?"

"And name it Wheaty, after your dog. The one you had when you were a little girl."

Mrs. Begley's heart began to pound. "Tell me, when is my birthday?"

"December tenth, silly."

"And who shares that birthday?"

"Well, Aunt Celia of course. And Mr. Brower, from Daddy's work. I remember because they went out drinking that time and forgot all about the party and we had to get a taxi and Grandpa said that he always had known that Daddy was trouble."

It was her. It was Emma.

"Emma," said Mrs. Begley. "Emma, my little girl. Talk to me, my darling."

"But I am talking. And Judie's reminding me to tell you that it wasn't her who pushed me. It was Jane. But Judie did break the branch off the lemon tree after you told us not to climb in it. That was you, Judie." Then she stopped and shook her head. "No, Judie. I'm not ready." The woman sighed and then looked sadly at Mrs. Begley. "I'm sorry, but Judie's coming back. She says she's tired."

"No," said Mrs. Begley. "I won't let you!" She grabbed the shot glass and hurled it across the room. The seated figure began to shake violently and she heard a pained "Mummy" escape the twisted mouth. "Mummy, I'm getting lost again."

Mrs. Begley grabbed the paper, crumpling it in her fist. She walked quickly to the stove and clicked the burner into a leaping flame. The paper was soon lit, flaring bright, and she dropped it, still flaming, into the sink. "There," she said to herself. "There. It's done."

It was done. She had done it. But what exactly?

Mrs. Begley looked to the table. She was filled with a painful awareness, but her reason was in a state of stasis, neither accepting nor denying. Sitting, knees splayed, was this woman. Her hair was ashy brown, streaked with gray. A great bosom heaved beneath the cashmere sweater. The eyes were tired at the edges, creases made prominent by caking liner. The mouth, smudged with lipstick, moved from a drooping purse to a smile, revealing teeth stained red with wine. The skin beneath the chin hung loose in a wattle and the hands, now reaching out to her, were wrinkled and mottled, fat digits adorned with garish purple paint.

"Mummy," said the creature. "Mummy, can we go home now? There is so much I want to do."

Apartment 4D

W e were sitting around the fire, which is what one did on Christmas Eve, and we had talked about all the happy stuff—that Henry had gotten into Wesleyan, his first choice, and that *Jarvis v. Lee* had finally, after nearly a decade, been brought to a conclusion. I had made out like a bandit on that one. We were now all going to Petra. "To Petra!" we said, toasting with eggnog, all except for Robert, who was on another health kick and met my glass with a ceramic tumbler of iced mate. But we always made that toast with each financial victory and Robert always countered with the same joke: "See Petra and die might be literal in our cases, Nida, if we wait much longer."

Sarah was graduating in another semester and said she was delighted to be done with college, but she was already burdened with premature nostalgia and had a little too much available wisdom for Henry's liking. She had lined up a job with a graphic design firm, one at which she'd held an internship the winter before. Excited, Sarah was moving to Brooklyn into an apartment with former schoolmates who had already graduated, as one of them was defecting to medical school in California come fall.

"I'm sharing with three other people," she said. "And there's a mouse problem."

"Mice?" I rolled my eyes and took a moment to think. "You kids have it good."

Henry said, "You always say, 'You kids have it good,' when you want to tell us how bad you had it."

"Ah, true." My son read my thoughts like cue cards. "It is a good story, although a bit gruesome for Christmas Eve."

"Then it's perfect," said Sarah. And I composed my thoughts.

———— ✦ ————

I'd been living with college friends since I'd graduated, but I wanted my own apartment. As you know, I was working as a paralegal then, so I couldn't afford to move, although I had engaged a realtor just in case. After several months, she found something within my range—a miracle, she said, adding that it wouldn't last long. I quickly made the deposit and soon I was packing my things.

I moved to the Cedar Arms, a place with no cedars and no arms that was, as the realtor put it, "in transition," as was the neighborhood. There was a hopeful café on a nearby corner once occupied by a bodega—it was called the Bodega Café—and here the other pioneers showed up with their laptops, ordering caramel lattes and gluten-free pastries, but gentrification was taking its time. The Cedar Arms' facade was composed of industrial brick and projected an ochre gloom into the street, an odd pocket of quiet that seemed sometimes peaceful, sometimes uncanny. The elevator didn't work and the stairwells and hallways were painted a peach color that had faded as it aged and was now a jaundiced flesh tone that clung unevenly to the pitted cinderblock walls. The sound bounced along the corridors and up the stairwells. You could never be sure which apartment was creating the noise—slamming pans on stove tops, slamming doors, suspicious thuds that could have been bodies slamming into walls but also could have been anything.

My apartment had been refurbished. The slatted blinds on the windows were new but cheap and sharp at the edges. You could cut your finger on one if you weren't careful. The walls were painted a glaring refrigerator-interior white. Friends had helped me move in, braving the stairs with my boxes and plants. One recommended I add a lock to the two already present. One recommended I move out as soon as my lease was up. One joked about the realtor's pointing out my luck in having a "park view," as my windows looked out on a muddy patch of land where the dog walkers' charges relieved themselves in a steady succession of canine leg raises and squats. There was a swing set there played upon by some determined children. It looked sturdy enough, but the joyless squeak and grind when it was in use made it seem unsafe. Even the occasional laughter of the kids—sometimes as many as twelve—who congregated beneath my window had an edge to it.

But there were advantages to living at the Cedar Arms. Best of all, it was an easy walk to the train. On a good day, I could get to work in forty minutes. Because the area was mostly occupied by low-income families, the groceries were cheap. Also, many people had dogs, and their regular circuits of the neighborhood made it safe. Those were the advantages, but the Cedar Arms was lonely. I had no friends living nearby and my job kept me at my desk for a solid nine hours every day. By the time I got home, I was loathe to venture out again, except on weekends. I had always thought myself a person who craved solitude, but after the first week, I began to see that isolation came with a creeping despair that any number of podcasts, complicated meals, and ferocious tidying could not offset.

If I'd run in to any of my neighbors, I would have introduced myself. I wasn't even sure who lived on my floor. Any encounters happened by the front entrance and were usually rushed—brief interactions with mothers with three children, hauling groceries and strollers, who were grateful when I held the door for them and thanked me but didn't have time for niceties. Once, I had seen the door to 4D, down the hall from me, open a crack then widen to reveal a thin girl of about ten with red-rimmed eyes. I'd smiled and said hello, but she'd chosen not to respond, and the door's aperture had slowly narrowed until it closed with a soft click.

I knew that there were apartment buildings where people never met their neighbors and had already decided to take my friend's advice and move as soon as possible, so I made peace with the situation. One week slipped into two.

When one evening there was a knocking at the door, I was at first scared. Any friend would have texted first and would need to be buzzed in. I approached the peephole. Standing in the hallway, looking directly into the door's eye, was a tiny woman with thick glasses and pulled-back hair. She wore a heavy cardigan, even though it was a warm day. I clicked through the two locks and pulled open the door.

"Hello," I said politely. "Can I help you?"

"Sure," said the woman. "You've just moved in and I'm here to welcome you. I'm Dora. I live down the hall." She stared around me into the apartment.

"I'm Nida," I said. "It's so nice of you to stop by. Would you like some tea? Or a coffee." I gestured at the Nespresso unit on the kitchen counter.

Dora walked inside and looked at the coffee machine. She smiled. "This is a nice apartment," she said. She pulled a chair from the dinette set and settled into it, placing her handbag on the table. "Young people usually have beer."

"Not this young person," I responded. I guessed Dora was somewhere in her seventies. "Would you settle for wine? Red wine?"

"If it's not too much trouble."

"Bottle's already open."

Dora had lived at the Cedar Arms for nearly fifty years and was one of the original tenants. She had a daughter who'd grown up there, was now living somewhere else, and who at some point was going to bring Dora to live with her.

It hadn't happened yet and Dora wasn't sure how she felt about it.

"This place has been going downhill ever since I got here," she said. "But then you move in . . ." I had a feeling she wanted to know how much I was paying for rent.

Dora knew the old-timers in the building. She had a regular *Wheel of Fortune* date with Shirley, who lived on the third floor. And she'd been friends with the man who had occupied my apartment.

"What happened to him?" I asked.

"Ed. We all used to call him Red Ed, because he had some kind of skin condition. Well, he's gone now." For the older tenants, the place was rent controlled, and I had the uncomfortable feeling that Red Ed had died in my apartment, but Dora wasn't up to divulging yet. I had more wine, so I bided my time. I asked her about the others along the hallway, and even she didn't know all of them.

"I try," she said. "But I've said more to you just now than some in five years. And a lot of people aren't here that long."

"I did see a little girl two doors down. I said hello, but she just ignored it. Maybe she's not allowed to talk to strangers."

"The girl's name is Mariah," Dora informed me. "And her mother is Heather. And there's something wrong there. I used to hear the mother screaming all the time. I called social services, which I never do, but that's how bad it was."

"That's funny. I haven't heard anything at all."

"Maybe that mother pulled herself together. I did talk to her once, before that, and she didn't seem an angry kind of person, just really sad, but if you'd heard her yelling. Scary."

"And it's just the two of them?"

"Around here, it's mostly just mothers. Like me." Dora smiled. "My Stan said he was just going round the corner and that was it."

"He never came back?"

"He might yet. It's been fifty years, but you never know." Dora chuckled and pushed her empty wineglass in my direction.

It turned out that Red Ed had indeed died in my apartment. The neighbors had caught the smell days before but thought it was something that had expired in the walls. Some speculated that it was 4D, because Heather would often let bags of rubbish collect outside her door. But the smell, unlike most things, became impossible to ignore. They had taken Red Ed out on a stretcher and then the stacks of comics and newspapers and accumulated soup cans out in trash bags, and that had been it.

"Although that smell stuck around. We used to say, 'Ed, enough already. You have overstayed your welcome.'"

My apartment was empty for over a year. They pulled out all the carpet and a wall in the bedroom, but the smell persisted. Ed had died in November and throughout that winter, the residents of the Cedar Arms left their windows cracked—their breath visible as they made their dinners and watched TV wrapped to their chins in blankets. And then the smell was gone.

"I don't believe in ghosts," said Dora, "but that smell—made you believe in something."

Dora laughed. She caught my nervous look. "You don't have to worry about Ed," she said. "He was a happy man and he lived a full life."

"But that detail about the soup cans is kind of sad," I said.

"What can I say?" said Dora. "Ed really loved soup."

A few weeks passed and I began to develop a routine. On Tuesdays, I joined Dora and Shirley for *Wheel of Fortune*, bringing wine and staying for Dora's mac and cheese and Shirley's butterscotch squares. Shirley was younger, in her late fifties, but had bad emphysema, and I started helping the ladies with their shopping. I didn't mind. They were both scrupulous with their accounting, paying what was owed to the last penny. I even started getting to know some of the children, little girls who liked my outfits, boys who wanted to know what was in my satchel. Every now and then I'd buy them a bag of Starburst, for which they were always grateful; sometimes they even remembered to thank me. But Mariah from 4D was seldom with them, and even when she was, she seemed to hang back. To me, Mariah looked malnourished, but I didn't know children and wondered if some were just thin. My privilege made me question myself, my judgment. And then one hot day I was passing by the kids on the way back from the dumpster when I felt a stream of water hit between my shoulder blades. I spun around. It was Mariah, and she was holding the hose, which she then lowered. The kids had been squirting each other with it, which they weren't supposed to do but had seemed reasonable enough given the day's temperature.

"Don't do that," I said. "It's not nice." I was in a bad mood because of the heat and work and a boyfriend that had turned out not to be a boyfriend, and this put me on edge. I turned to leave and again she hit me with the hose, and this time as I turned she didn't lower it but instead kept squirting me.

"Stop it!" I said.

But she kept the stream trained on me as I strode up and grabbed the hose from her. The other children grew quiet and watchful.

"Apologize," I said. "Apologize right now."

Mariah looked into my eyes with somber, unblinking interest.

"If you don't say you're sorry, I'm going to march you upstairs and talk to your mother."

Mariah didn't move.

"All right," I said. I grabbed her by the wrist, her bones as sharp and light as a bird's, and headed to the building. Mariah didn't fight me at first, but as we neared the entrance, she shook her arm until I let her go. Her eyes went up to the fourth floor, where I saw her mother standing at the window watching us.

"What are you looking at?" asked Mariah.

"I'm looking at your mother," I said.

Mariah's eyes narrowed and she fixed me with a penetrating, disquieting look. "You can't talk to her."

"Why not?"

"I'm going to get in trouble. She's . . ." Mariah struggled to articulate. "She's not like other mothers."

I felt a chill go over me. "Then apologize and we can stop this."

Mariah considered. "I shouldn't have squirted you with the hose."

"Thank you," I said. I wanted to leave it at that, but somehow it seemed wrong. "Why did you do it?" I asked.

"Because I wanted you to see me." She dropped her eyes then, and I thought she might be feeling some variety of shame but no. She looked up again directly into my face and said, "I like your shoes."

The shoes in question were pink suede Converse platform sneakers. I thought about this as I made the steps to the fourth floor. The girl's behavior had been strange, but I also thought that I should probably knock on the door of 4D and apologize to the woman for manhandling her daughter. I wondered what Mariah could have meant when she said that Heather wasn't like other mothers and if I was indeed going to get her into trouble. The look I'd seen on the mother's face, although from far away, hadn't exactly been tender.

I walked up the stairs and to the door of 4D, my hand drawn into a fist and ready to knock, when I heard sobbing from deep inside the apartment. I pressed my ear to the door and listened. The crying sounded as if it was coming from the far side, from right by the window. I thought to knock gently, although she might not hear. I could explain that it wasn't all that bad. Just a misunderstanding, a little girl who liked shoes and didn't know how to ask about them. I tapped and the sobbing suddenly stopped. Then I heard from just the other side of the door a voice: "You need to leave now." I pulled back, startled that she could have crossed the room so quickly. Was it a different woman? I made my way to my apartment, entering in such a rush that I slammed the door behind me.

For the next couple of weeks, I didn't see Mariah, not with the other kids, not in the hallway. And I didn't see Heather. When I exited the apartment, I moved quickly, not wanting to run into either of them. Dora wasn't surprised by this, because she said she'd felt that way for quite some time, but I was rattled. I didn't like being alone in my rooms and had started talking to myself as a way of filling up the space. Then one day I was coming home from work and I saw Mariah crouching at the far side of the building. Her back was turned to me, but she was shaking a little, and I thought she was crying. I considered going over to her, but I was tired and had decided to pass when I heard a mewling. She seemed to have a kitten. I walked along the side of the building until I was close, watching her shaking back, wondering what was wrong, when the kitten—still unseen—gave a sad and anguished meow that ended in a hiss.

"Mariah," I said. When she turned, I'd expected to see her face in tears, but she was smiling. The shaking of her back had been laughter not crying. "Mariah, what are you doing to that kitten?"

"We're playing," she said.

"You're going to have to stop." I drew closer, although being near her felt unnatural. The kitten was tiny and white, with a pink nose and barely open eyes. It meowed again. Mariah went to grab the kitten, but it slid beneath the hedge out of reach.

"You scared it," she said.

"Please move."

"Why?"

"I'd like to help the kitten."

"The kitten's mine."

We locked eyes. "Do you want me to ask your mother if that's true?"

As before, at the mention of her mother, the girl listened. Mariah stepped aside. The kitten continued to meow, softer now. I felt that its pleas were sounding in my brain. I knelt on the ground and parted the low branches of the shrub. The kitten blinked at me, quivering pathetically, and

I reached in and grabbed it. It was a handful of tiny bones, damp fur, a madly skittering heart.

"I'll take care of it, Mariah. Go home."

"That's not your cat."

"It's no one's cat. But I'm going to make sure it's safe, all right?"

Mariah had no choice but to listen. She slipped along the side of the building like a shadow and entered the Cedar Arms noiselessly, letting the door close softly behind her. I'd been so absorbed in watching her that I'd failed to notice the change in the kitten, who was no longer shivering but now purring as it warmed up in my hands.

Dora, who had to watch the kitten during the day, named her Egypt.

"Why Egypt?"

"Because," said Dora. "I always wanted to go to Egypt."

Dora was now keeping an eye out for Mariah. She worried about the girl. Kids that messed with animals were usually abused themselves. And while Heather seemed harmless enough, when was the last time anyone had talked to her? When someone avoided people to that degree, it had to be drinking or *the drugs*, as Dora always said. I wondered when Heather did her shopping, but Dora and Shirley were mostly confined to their apartments and I was mostly at work, so why would we see her hauling the bags?

Truth was I did see Heather. I would see her watching me from her window when I took out the trash. One morning, when I was leaving for work, she was standing idly in the hallway, wearing gray sweatpants, a dingy white T-shirt, and a yellow terrycloth bathrobe. Even though she was often only ten or twelve feet away, I couldn't bring myself to speak to her. She also did not speak but just looked at me intently as if I were supposed to understand what that look meant. She didn't appear to be drunk, but maybe she was—something seemed off—and I continued past her.

As the weeks went by, Egypt grew stronger, although I had a feeling she would always be small. She learned the drill, and in the mornings would follow me down the corridor to Dora's apartment. When I returned in the evening, she would be waiting for me at Dora's door, always knowing when I was about to show up. Mariah and Heather slipped from my mind. Work was busy and having a pet dispelled the anxiety from the stillness of my apartment. Then one evening, in the fading light, I happened to be looking out the window and saw Mariah standing alone in the rain. Her back was to me, but I could see that she was looking at a pigeon that was pecking intently at a patch of earth a short distance away. Mariah raised her hand and threw something expertly—a rock?—and hit the pigeon, which fell over and was still. Mariah picked up the bird, which might have been dead or just stunned. I was trying to figure this out when she looked up at the windows of the fourth floor. I ducked behind the frame, but she wasn't looking at me. She was looking at her own window I think. She must have been looking at her mother.

I stood by my door, just open a crack, watching for Mariah. When she crossed my line of vision, she did so quickly, as if sensing she was being watched, and then ducked into her apartment. I scooped up Egypt and went down the hall to talk to Dora.

"What do we do?" I asked.

"I'm going to call social services again," she said.

"What are you going to say? That we think she killed a pigeon?"

"I'll think of something," said Dora.

Close to a week later, a young woman from social services showed up. It was a Friday and I was home early—some Fridays they let us go after lunch—so I was there when Dora knocked on my door with the woman, who looked to be about my age. She had been trying to reach Heather by phone, but the service had been cut off for lack of payment a couple of months before, and so she made the trip. The building manager—a man I'd never seen before—was with them, looking bored and annoyed. "They're fine," he said. "They don't complain," he added, leveling a less than civil look in Dora's direction.

"So what's the problem?" the social worker asked.

"The girl looks malnourished," I said. "And she's been behaving strangely."

There was a moment when we all looked at each other, unsatisfied for different reasons.

"Can we just check on her?" I asked. "You're here anyway," I added, addressing the social worker, who was carrying a bag jammed with files.

"Okay," she said.

We went down the hall to 4D and knocked. There was no answer.

I said, "Mariah might be in there and not answering."

"How old is she?" asked the social worker.

"The girl or the mother?" asked Dora.

"I think the girl is ten, but as she's in your care, you should probably know that," I said. The social worker gave me an assessing look, up and down my outfit and finally at my face. She was unimpressed.

"I have fifty cases," the social worker said. "Twenty of them I inherited from my predecessor, who was fired last week. This is one of those cases."

"Why was she fired?" asked Dora.

"Well maybe," said the social worker, "she didn't remember the age of one of the children in her caseload."

I wasn't exactly chastened, but I was beginning to understand. "Sorry," I said. "I should be more . . ." I couldn't think of the word. I wasn't grateful. Maybe the correct word was "surprised," surprised that she'd cared enough to show up. "Thank you for coming."

The social worker sighed and then shrugged to the manager, and he produced a key and opened the door. "Just lock it behind you when you're done," he said and left.

Dora grabbed my elbow and pulled me along with her into the apartment, although I would have been content to stay in the hallway. I was preparing for a sense of dread as I entered that space, for the air to sing with some ominous foreboding, but it was the stillness—the mundanity—of the place that put me off. Yes, it was untidy but not terribly so. And this might have been because of the lack of objects. There were no magazines stacked on the coffee table because there were no magazines. Clearly the place could have used a vacuum, but there seemed to be little traffic there, and the dirtiness was more a layer of dust that settled sadly in an absence of clutter.

I walked around the couch, which was upholstered in an industrial, itchy-looking beige fabric, to look out the window. The pane was covered in a gauze of dust, but I could see a pair of handprints and then another. They must have been Heather's because they were high up on the glass and not that different in size from my own hands—I held mine over the outlines—but with longer fingers.

"Dirty dishes in the sink," said Dora, as if it were a crime. She flipped on the lights in the kitchenette.

"You shouldn't be in here," the social worker called from the bedroom.

I'd come to stand by Dora, who had her hands in little fists on her hips and was swinging her gaze around the kitchen like a lighthouse beam. She gestured at the counter. "And this is the tiniest chicken carcass I ever saw."

At this point, the social worker had had enough and was ready to evict us. She stomped into the kitchen and we three stared at the bird skeleton, picked clean of flesh. Had they roasted it? Boiled it?

"I've seen worse," said the social worker.

"Really?" I said. "Because that's a pigeon. I saw the girl kill it. And now I know why."

Where another person might have been defensive, the social worker was intrigued. She gave us her card. Her name was Angela Diaz.

She said, "I'm going to dig around, see if there's anything in the file."

A month or so passed, with no news on Mariah and Heather, and nothing to report. One of my close friends, Nell, had gotten engaged and become insufferable as she planned her wedding. She assumed my antipathy stemmed from the fact that I'd had a long-term relationship fall apart a year earlier, but I'd gotten over it. Honestly, Nell's anger toward me seemed odd and then I began to think that her relationship—which had always seemed strained to me—was actually toxic. I bowed out of planning the shower, stating that I was just too busy, to which Nell replied, "Nida's too busy hanging out with her cat and watching *The Golden Girls* with the grannies."

It was true. I did prefer being with Dora and Shirley. To Nell, I seemed unhealthy. I wasn't really dating, unless you counted Grant, a guy my age in an open marriage that wasn't his idea, who accompanied me to lunches and galleries on the weekends so that he could tell his wife he'd been on a date. I'd grown tired of keeping up, tired of the hectic loneliness of being in my twenties, of not having a real profession, of haunting wine bars and brunch spots and bleeding money I didn't have. I'd met Dora's daughter, who was my mother's age, and she was nice, happy to meet me, had even said that her mother loved cats and now had one that someone else looked after. My family, as you know, was in distant Illinois and this family—Dora, Egypt, and Shirley—needed me. I'd even learned to crochet and with Shirley's help was making an afghan. I joked with my friends that I'd retired. Some said they were jealous but didn't mean it, and some said they were jealous and sounded sincere.

One night I was making my weekly pilgrimage to the dumpster and looked up and saw Mariah watching me from her window. I waved to her and she waved back. I wondered if Angela had managed to connect with Heather, because that wave seemed significant. Then I saw Heather come and stand behind Mariah. This was the first time I'd seen the two of them together, and this, too, had to mean something.

But as I was walking up the hall to my apartment, I was surprised to hear arguing in 4D and paused outside the door. I heard Mariah's agitated voice. She was whispering angrily. She said, "Why don't you leave me alone? You're a bad mother. Bad." And then she said, "I'll find a better mother." Or at least I think that's what she said. Her voice had dropped to a whisper.

A few weeks later, I was in my apartment paying bills when Egypt began clawing at the door. I left the table and peered through the peephole. There was a woman standing there but facing down the hall so I could only see the back of her head, the hair lank and greasy, and then she turned, startling me. It was Heather. She looked anxious, disheveled, still in the same sweatpants and yellow robe. She backed down the hall, and I could see now that her shirt was stained with something that might have been blood, and there was blood too on her hands. From the panic in her face and her pleading eyes, I felt that something terrible had happened. She seemed in shock, uncomposed, sort of shaking in place, then taking wobbly steps. My first instinct was to slide down the door and hide, but I pulled myself together and unlocked each of the locks. But when I looked out, she was gone. Down the hallway, the door to apartment 4D was open just a sliver, and as I watched, it closed with a barely audible click.

I took Egypt in my arms and stepped into the hallway. There was no one there. I closed my door, locking it, dropped my keys in my pocket, and went down the hall. Dora was, as usual, at home. She had her scrapbook project spread across the table, and the TV was on with *Little House on the Prairie* playing at a low volume. Dora looked me up and down and took Egypt, setting her on the floor.

"What's wrong?" she said.

"I saw Heather outside my apartment and she had blood on her T-shirt, on her hands." Dora's eyes widened. "When I finally got my courage up and opened the door, she was gone."

"Back in her apartment?"

"I saw her door click shut, but when I was watching her, she looked on the point of collapse, like she could barely walk." I took the mugs from the drainer and set them on the counter. I dropped in the Red Rose teabags and filled the kettle. "So, do we call the police? I think we should. But I just have this weird feeling about it."

"Are you sure it was blood?"

I *had* been sure it was blood, which wasn't the same thing. "No."

Dora said, "Let's call Angela Diaz."

I watched Dora dial the number, but it went straight to voicemail. Dora handed me the phone. I said something about Heather's seeming disoriented, that someone should check on her. I didn't mention the blood. I didn't think I was jumping to conclusions, but I wasn't ready to appear to be seeing violence where there was none. It was a vague message and unsatisfying, clearly, as communicated to me by Dora's expression.

A few weeks passed. One Saturday, Dora was over for pancakes and bacon, which was a semiregular occurrence. Dora loved bacon, though she could never finish a whole pack herself and left it to me to provide her with it. Dora and I were making our goodbyes when we saw Angela in the hallway, lugging her usual exploding bag of files. She was attempting to fish something out of her coat pocket, while her eyes searched up and down the hallway.

"It's 4D," I said. "Maybe you could use a coffee first?"

Angela looked first at Dora and then at me, defeat registering on her face. "I could use a coffee," she said.

Angela took a seat at the dinette and looked around my living area. I saw her take in the plants, the shelves with books, the Frida Kahlo print, the neatly rolled yoga mat tucked upright in the corner. Angela usually worked weekends because that's when you could drop in on clients and see the kids. It seemed an unrewarding and thankless profession, but both Dora and I pretended there was hope because it seemed rude not to. I set the Nespresso unit to grinding out a coffee.

I told Angela about the state I'd seen Heather in, her agitation and the stains on her clothes. "That was weeks ago." Angela sat attentively, but I saw how much patience it was requiring her to listen.

"I think you should check on Mariah," I said. "I haven't seen her in a while."

"You think Mariah's dead?"

I hadn't said as much, had been coyly skirting the bald assertion even to myself. I said, "Heather seemed very agitated."

Angela dropped her head for a second and then looked up first at me and then at Dora. "You seem to be good people and I'm not supposed to share this information, but if I do, will you leave me alone? And them alone?" She gestured toward the door, which included the tenants down the hall in 4D and possibly the rest of the world. "Heather is struggling, but she's not a bad person. There are many standards of parenting."

"What do you mean?" I asked.

"Look, Heather has no record of violence. She was having a rough time a year or so ago." I glanced over at Dora, who was thinking *the drugs*. "Heather said she wanted to put Mariah in foster care. But she worked it out."

"She wanted to put Mariah in foster care? Why?"

"I've already said too much." Angela's eyes narrowed.

"But where is Mariah now?" I asked.

"I contacted the school. She's been in class, hasn't missed a day in weeks."

So Mariah was okay.

"It's because they feed her there, breakfast and lunch," said Dora.

"Well, then," said Angela. "The girl is eating."

"So if everything's so hunky-dory," I asked, "why are you here?"

"Just checking in on Heather and letting you know that you can chill out. Instead of some kind of surveillance, what that woman needs is friends."

Dora and I weren't exactly cowed. Something was up, even though I did not know what that something was. We watched Angela knocking on the door of 4D, and we must have looked smug enough when there was no answer. Dora set her mouth in a firm, straight line. "I'm not nosy," she said.

I looked at her.

"I am not," she insisted.

I resolved to leave Mariah and Heather to their life, and Dora, too, was doing her best to keep them from our conversations. I did see Heather once, slipping across the hallway, and she fixed me with a look of such aggravated despair that I wondered if Angela had mentioned to her what Dora and I had said, our concerns that now seemed like gossip.

"I'm Nida," I said finally, because what else could I say? Heather did not respond. There was something unnatural in the set of her shoulders, and her unmoving expression made me incapable of saying more, of staying in the hallway with its flickering bulb and stale, moldy air. I retreated to my apartment, but the encounter unsettled me. I hadn't seen Mariah in a long time and wondered if maybe the school had made a mistake, had gotten her confused with another child, which seemed easy to do, but it wasn't my business and no one wanted it to be. Although it did cross my mind that Red Ed had also been no one's business, no one's until the odor of his death insinuated itself into the walls of the Cedar Arms, permeating the building's corridors until no one could deny that something was wrong. That smell had stayed as a disapprobation long after Ed's body had been removed. Maybe the lesson wasn't that we should know our neighbors better but rather that people suffered and sometimes died and there was nothing you could do about it.

I focused on work and applied for a promotion, which went to an outside hire, and so I resolved to go to law school. Egypt liked all the studying and would sit on my lap, stretching her paws into my book. I had little time to pointlessly ruminate. My visits to Dora were almost exclusively limited to when I dropped Egypt off and picked her up—and Saturday breakfast. Dora supported me. She wanted me to be a lawyer. She was proud of my efforts. The tenants of 4D receded from my thoughts until one Tuesday afternoon when, exhausted from work, I was unlocking my door and Mariah tapped me on the arm. And yes, I was startled and initially angry, but then I was just warily surprised. Had I really thought her dead? I stepped back and Mariah and I faced each other, that odd cloud of tension that followed her everywhere sitting over us both.

"Mariah," I said. "Is everything okay?"

"Why are you always alone?"

"Alone? I'm not always alone."

"You're alone now. Do you have a boyfriend?"

"Yes," I lied. I thought of Grant. In my mind's eye, he was waving at us unconvincingly.

"I've never seen him."

"Seeing isn't everything," I said. "How's your mother?" In addition to changing the topic, I actually did want to know.

Mariah smiled at me as if we shared a joke. She said, "She says hi."

The girl was fine. Perhaps her mother had emotional problems, but one had to admire Mariah. She was a survivor, and that was what I was thinking several days later as I locked my door to head down the hallway for a much-earned *Wheel of Fortune* study break.

"Come on, Egypt," I said, and she gave up licking her paw to trot down the hall, leading the way.

My head was full of the LSATs and scheduling and law schools, distracted with the complicated matter of the future, so when the door to 4D cracked open, I was not at first alarmed, just curious. Then Mariah's thin arms shot out and grabbed Egypt, pulled the cat in, and the door slammed shut.

I stood at the door, as if taunted by the metal 4D screwed into the panel, slightly skewed and dusted with corrosion. I knew that I had to go in, but I felt paralyzed. A few long seconds passed. On the other side of the door, all was quiet. Finally, I knocked on the door, then knocked louder, and when there was no answer, I opened it and stepped inside. Mariah was standing in the living room, Egypt struggling in her arms.

"I just wanted to give her some milk."

"Then you should ask me," I said.

"Can I give her some milk?" For the first time, Mariah looked vulnerable.

"Maybe another time," I said. I thought I heard something, a soft cry coming from the bedroom. Mariah's eyes flickered to the door, confirming it was real.

"Doesn't your cat like milk?" Mariah said. She put Egypt down, who trotted over to me and waited by the door. Mariah went to the fridge and opened it. She took out a small carton, the kind they give with school lunches, and I saw that there were several such cartons on the refrigerator shelves. She opened the carton deliberately, pouring some milk into a chipped blue bowl. I heard another noise, a soft sob, come from the bedroom again. The hairs on my arms began to prickle.

"Mariah, where is your mother?"

Mariah looked to the bedroom door, then back to me. "She's taking a nap."

The bowl on the counter began to shake and I watched it, unsure of what I was seeing. Then, as if guided by an invisible hand, the bowl slid off the counter and shattered on the floor.

"Why did you do that?" Mariah shouted. Her face fell and then recomposed itself in anger. Working hard, the girl calmed herself again. On the kitchen floor there were shards of blue ceramic in a milky puddle.

"There's more milk," Mariah said.

"Mariah, I think I should go."

"You don't understand," said Mariah. "No one understands."

I'd never seen someone so alone. "No one understands what?"

"She's not like other mothers," said Mariah. "She didn't want me. She was going to give me away."

"Your mother?" I don't know why I asked. Who else could it have been? The door to the bedroom then slammed open. *Wrong*, I thought, *wrong not real*. But regardless, the door *had* opened. I saw the bed unmade and no one lying in it. My heart was pounding, a pounding that I could feel against my ribs. I stepped back, resting my hand on the doorknob, and eased the door open. Egypt made a hasty escape.

"Don't go," said Mariah.

"I'll be back," I said. "I just want to tell Dora that Egypt and I are going to visit with you first. I don't want Dora to worry."

"No," said Mariah. She was frustrated, angry, and close to tears.

I cautiously opened the door farther, and Mariah was running at me, running with her tiny hands outstretched and a look of ferocious determination. The lights were flickering—I remember that—and then she was on me and the world went dark.

Apparently, I'd slipped and hit my head on the door, trying to get away. Or Mariah had knocked me over. Something had happened, but when Egypt showed up at Dora's without me, Dora came looking. She called the building manager and he'd forced the door open as it wasn't altogether shut and he could see me lying on the floor, blocking the entrance. Dora, who never called the police, had called the police. They searched the apartment because Mariah was missing, but in the closet, wrapped in a blanket, were the remains of a woman. The police thought she'd been there for at least a year.

I stood in the hallway by Dora's apartment, an ice pack held to the back of my head. Dora kept trying to get me to lie down, but my adrenaline was surging and I couldn't sit

still, so I stood swaying in the corridor as a detective pep-
pered me with questions to which I had few answers. "I don't
know who it is in that closet," I said. "But I saw Heather just
last week."

"Well, ma'am," said the detective, "we're pretty sure it's
her."

"That's ridiculous," I said. "It can't be her. Look."

Heather, in the same stained sweats and robe, was
standing by the door to 4D. She did not approach, which
struck me as odd. But everything about her just seemed so
strange, and I wondered what I should say to her or if I
should speak to her at all. Heather was watching me, her
face carved in sorrow but also with an emotion I couldn't
quite place. It might have been pride.

"That's Heather, just down the hall," I said.

The detective and policewoman followed my gaze but
quickly tracked back to looking fixedly at me.

"Ma'am," said the policewoman, "I think you need to
sit down."

"I'm fine," I said. The policewoman had a kindly,
interested expression but clearly was not paying attention.
I pointed so as not to be again, somehow, misunderstood.
"The woman standing right outside 4D is Mariah's mother.
Can't you see her?"

But when I looked to her again, she'd disappeared.

I've been piecing together the events of those months
ever since, and they shift and slide then come together in

different ways. I know what I saw, although sometimes the order of things is muddled, Heather's appearances rotating through my time at the Cedar Arms like face cards in an old, well-shuffled deck.

The fire needed to be stirred, but at first no one moved. Robert shook his head with smile, actually a smirk. "Quite a tale," he said.

Henry got up and tossed on another log. He disturbed it with the poker and turned to me.

"So what happened to Mariah?"

"Oh, they must have tracked her down, but they didn't see any need to inform me. I moved out two days later and that was that."

Henry's brows were drawn as he sorted through the narrative. "And the mother? How did you know—"

"Who knows exactly what happened to Heather?" I said. "She'd been dead a year when they found the body. They probably assumed it was an overdose or possibly a suicide."

"And that was it?" asked Sarah.

"In a manner of speaking. Maybe twelve years after that, Dora died. We'd stayed intermittently in touch. Birthday calls then Christmas cards. Her daughter let me know about the funeral. And I went. I was a stranger standing among the graves, a voice of the past, my past perhaps, and then I saw her."

"Mariah?" asked Henry.

"I think it was Mariah. It must have been. She had that same searching look, and her eyes settled on me. She was wearing an ankle-length camel hair coat and pink suede boots. Her hair was cropped short. I'd never thought her pretty, but she was. Beautiful even."

Remote Control

"I guess I can die now," she said.

"Why, because you've seen Monte?"

"Yeah. That's a thing."

"I'm quite sure it's not *a thing*, as you say. 'See Venice and die' is a thing."

"So what is it with Monte Carlo?"

They were on the Corniche, driving back to Mougins after a day's sightseeing. The traffic did not allow one to speed but given the opportunity she might have—like Princess Grace, who had, unfortunately, gone off the edge.

Carl considered. "I think what you are referring to is that line from *To Catch a Thief* where she says, 'I'd give my eyes to see Monte,' and he replies, 'That would rather defeat the purpose.'"

"But aren't they in Monte Carlo when she says that? Why would she say that if she was already in Monte Carlo?"

"I don't know. I haven't seen the film in thirty years. We'll have to watch it again when we get home."

Which is what people did. Went to a place because some film made it seem essential to one's life experience and then watched the film again to remember . . . what? To remember that one had been right to want to go there? They had done the same with *A Room with a View* after going to Florence. And they had been right to go to Florence. And they had been right to go to Monte Carlo, even if it had just been for the day. Life seemed to move forward on these little loops.

"Wait a minute," she said. "I don't think that line is from *To Catch a Thief*. Isn't it from *Rebecca*?"

"You could be right," Carl said.

"Sometimes I am." She wrinkled her nose at him. Carl was twenty-two years older and that was definitely *a thing*.

She drove along the narrow road with the shoulder of the mountain projecting above her. In the perfect blue waters small yachts bobbed, and rich people—who seemed to have been generated from a collective middle-class imagination—strolled the promenade in long shorts and sunglasses, in dresses whipping in the breeze, doing their bit for the view. "Look at that Rolls," she said. "Look at the gate. Who lives behind a gate like that?"

The exchange was from *Rebecca*. She'd googled it when they got back to the villa. She let Carl know as she assembled the serrano ham and baguette and cheese that would be their dinner.

"Mrs. Van Hopper says, 'Most girls would give their eyes to see Monte,' and Max de Winter responds, 'That would kind of defeat the purpose.'"

"Ah," he said. "And now that we know that, what else is there to know?"

They brought their dinner to the terrace by the pool. The property they'd rented, a villa a ten-minute drive to the village of Mougins, was built on a series of terraces and offered views down the mountain, a dive punctuated by cypresses and other bristling, less vertical trees. As the day faded, lights from the other houses began to twinkle. The heat was stirred by a docile breeze. "We should swim after we eat," she said.

He tried to get the lights on in the pool, but he couldn't get them to work. This was added to a list of things that needed attention. The Wi-Fi was so slow as not to be functioning. There were only two forks. The television kept coming on at a blasting volume at 2:00 a.m.—or had for the last two nights, since they'd arrived. They had no idea where to put the trash. Carl called the owner, who would drop by in the morning.

Their bedroom was up a set of spiral stairs that led from the living room and had its own bathroom. Another suite of rooms was accessed by steps to the left of the front door. The layout was mazelike. Several times she had found herself in the laundry instead of the entry hall when trying to go outside. The house was too big for two people, but Carl had selected it for the pool (he'd said that she needed a pool) and as they'd booked late and he wanted to be within striking distance of Nice, it was the best option. For a house this size with these amenities and in this location, the rent was surprisingly reasonable. The maintenance was a bit lax but hardly substandard. Some shrubs could have used a pruning and there were piles of leaves blown up against the walls of the house, but she liked that. The nod to wildness seemed authentic, a part of the contrasts, as was the herd of goats that grazed in the field behind the house.

She had been sound asleep, her head on Carl's shoulder, when the television came on. At first she didn't know where she was. Why all the yelling in French?

"Carl," she said. "Carl, the TV's on again."

He mumbled in his sleep, but it didn't seem worth rousing him. She got up, pulling on Carl's robe—he always traveled with a robe—and flicked the stairwell light on. The floor felt cold beneath her feet. In the living room, the TV was splashing light against the walls. The show was a comedy set in what looked to be the antebellum South. She picked up the remote from the coffee table. Just as she was about to turn the television off, she felt eyes on her and looked down the hallway to her left. She thought she saw someone. A figure. Some solid shadow in a murky dark. She managed the steps to the light switch and turned it on. No one was there. She turned off the television and stood in the quiet listening. Of course it was silent. She turned off the living room light and made quick steps back up the winding stair. She would tell Carl in the morning that the 2:00 a.m. TV blasting made her nervous. She would tell him that she thought she saw someone in the hallway. She would tell him these things, she thought, as she slid into bed beside him, and he would laugh, amazed at just how illogical and emotional she could be. Carl attributed this to her youth, but that's just how she was. She would not age out of it.

"You say it looked like a shadow."

"Yes."

"If it looked most like a shadow, then it was most likely a shadow."

This was hard to argue with, particularly as she wanted it to be true.

Today, they were going to the beach in Antibes. Originally, they had planned on an early start, but she woke late after having had a hard time getting back to sleep the previous night. Then they needed supplies and a trip to the village had to be made and, of course, the bakery was sold out of almond croissants. The expression of the woman behind the counter made it clear she thought they were mad. Who would try to buy a croissant at 11:00 a.m.? The woman directed them to the Casino Supermarket as they seemed the sort of people who might actually eat a baked good purchased there. The exchange was hilarious and she imitated the woman, repeating, "Croissant? A cette heur?" several times with increasing horror.

Carl smiled and took stock of her, his eyes pointed and amused. "Iola would have been so offended. And you don't care." Iola was Carl's ex-wife.

"Ask why I don't care."

"Why don't you care?"

"Because it doesn't matter. And because that woman was really, really funny."

Carl hardly mentioned Iola, and she seldom asked about Iola as it seemed the sort of thing that new wives did that was—or would be—beneath her. She felt pressured to be confident because of the age difference. Being secure in one's self seemed the thing a more mature wife would be. She did not know what that felt like, but she did know what it looked like.

By the time they parked the car and reached the beach, it was two o'clock and the sun just a hole in the sky, a portal to an overflowing vat of heat. They bought ice creams and ate them at record speed. They set out their towels with the edges touching other people's towels, but no one was upset. They swam in the salty, tepid water, around standing bathers with poached brains, through the wakes of breast strokers, out to the ropes where the water was a touch cooler. They hung on a buoy. Just beyond were the yachts. She looked out to sea, but she could feel his eyes on her.

"Don't tell me you love me," she said.

"Why not?"

"Because you're deranged with heat and it won't count."

The drive back to the villa was up a steep, narrow road. There were several hairpin turns as they made their ascent and sometimes the tires skidded trying to find traction on patches of gravel. Their villa was one of two at the end of the road, and they had yet to encounter another car on this final stretch. The metal gate swung open with a remote control. The drive to the house was shared with the one neighbor and after the car was parked in the garage, they unlocked the first gate that led to the public path, locked that behind them, then unlocked the second gate that led to house, and locked that behind them. The door to the house was enforced with decorative beaten copper and they unlocked that as well. Finally inside, Carl made straight for the refrigerator.

"Let's have some champagne," he said.

With mock horror, she responded, "A cette heur?"

Then they heard a knock at the door. It was the owner of the house. Together they wandered around and watched as he reset the Wi-Fi and explained the mystery of operating the pool lights. There was also a gas grill, and this, too, was shown to function after a few simple tasks, including—significantly—opening the valve of the tank. They returned to the house.

"What about the TV?" she asked.

The man quickly turned the television on, showing her the remote.

"It comes on every night at two," she said. She gestured for Carl to explain, which he did. The man shrugged, not understanding. He and Carl went back and forth with no improvement. She understood the man to say, in the end, that the television did not come on at two every night. Perhaps as there was no explanation, this seemed the only thing to say.

Sure enough, that night the TV came on again at 2:00 a.m. precisely. This time she made Carl go and deal with it, which he did. He made no mention of anyone lurking in the hallway. "The remote control must be short circuiting, or maybe there's some sort of timer function that's accidentally been activated. Who knows? Maybe it's picking up the signal from one of the neighbors."

The following day they had meant to drive to Éze to see the path famous for inspiring Nietzsche to write *Thus Spoke Zarathustra*, but as the day edged to noon, neither of them had made a move. She was in the pool, her elbows resting on the side, as Carl, lounging in the shelter of an umbrella, scrolled through his phone. "I haven't read *Thus Spoke Zarathustra*," she said.

"What?" Carl looked up.

"I haven't read *Thus Spoke Zarathustra*. Don't you think I should before we go to Éze? That way I can get the most out of seeing Nietzsche's path."

"Change of plan. You do whatever you're doing, I'll do whatever I'm doing, and we'll have dinner in the village."

The reservation was for eight and while he was in the shower, she went to have a cigarette on the terrace. That she was married seemed impossible. She was thinking of this when she was hailed by a woman passing on the path below her.

"Bon soir!" the woman said. And then a number of very friendly things with her hands flying around like dove wings. She had two terriers with her who were terribly well-behaved.

"Je suis desolez, mais je ne parle pas l'Francaise," she said. She shook her head, disappointed in her shortcoming.

"Ah," said the woman. There was a moment as she thought. "This good house too vacant. Now you here are very beautiful with your nice man. Is very good for this day. And happy."

"Thank you very much," she said. "And my man is very nice. And I'm not very beautiful, but thanks anyway. And I like you and your dogs." She giggled.

"Before," said the woman, making sure of the meaning by gesturing behind her head, "no peoples. The house no peoples. Much time."

"But why?" she asked. "It's such a nice house."

The woman shrugged emphatically. It was a mystery.

*   *   *

She and Carl had been married for six months, after a three-month courtship. Theirs was a ridiculous story. Or a romantic story. Or a scandal. Carl had been Zack's supervisor during his internship at Christie's. Zack had been her boyfriend and when he proposed that she join him in London, she couldn't refuse. Carl had hosted a dinner party and invited Zack, and she was Zack's "plus one." Predictably, her dress had been inappropriately casual, and nervous, she had started telling funny stories. Somewhere into the first hour of the party, she felt Zack's eyes on her. He was not having fun. He came up beside her as they walked into the dining room and said, "Thanks for putting the 'loud' in 'American' for me." When they were seated, Zack had pointedly moved her wineglass out of easy reach. She was silent through dinner, something noted—and understood—by Carl. She was so rattled by Zack that she thought she might start crying but held it together. As they were leaving, Carl put his hand on her shoulder and said, quietly, "Perhaps we could have lunch later this week?" He had written down his phone number. She looked at the scrap of paper. It was like something from a fortune cookie.

The village of Mougins spiraled down a mountain top. Picasso had lived there and the town was devoted to art, which it manifested in increasingly bizarre civic artworks that would no doubt have made Picasso ill. Together they walked arm in arm through the cobbled paths with other gawping couples, pausing at paintings that were embarrassing in their soft cubism, in their pandering kitsch, in their even values and fields that cared not for light or life or meaning. The restaurant was in a small plaza with a fountain. Parents walked children eating ice cream. Carl didn't like the reserved table as it was set in too far and insisted the host find one reached by the breeze, which the host did, swayed by Carl's fluent French and the fact that he seemed a person accustomed to the best. Carl ordered a bottle of Sancerre and some escargot and foie gras to start.

"When were you last in Mougins?" she asked.

"Oh, years ago."

"Why?"

"Why was I here?" He paused. "I was on holiday."

"With Iola?"

"Yes. With Iola."

"Why did you want to bring me here?"

"Because I like Mougins," he said.

"For the art?"

"No," he said with patience. He picked up his menu and began to look over the offerings. If there was a steak, he'd order that and ask that it come bloody. "I wanted you to see Mougins. It's a beautiful place. Don't you agree?"

"Yes," she said. She wanted to be agreeable, then decided that being dishonest about her thoughts wasn't worth it. "Were you on your honeymoon?"

Just then the waiter arrived with the wine and Carl was offered a glass to taste that he swirled, sipped, and approved with a subtle nod. When the waiter left, she was still looking at Carl, waiting for an answer.

"You don't need to compete with Iola. You could not be more different."

"And she's dead," she said. "But when she was alive, she was beautiful and sophisticated."

"You are beautiful," he said. "And you choose not to be sophisticated because you don't see the point of it." He was measuring his thoughts. "As you know, Iola died in a car accident. What you don't know is that she was with another man, someone that I worked with. He was driving and they went off a cliff. His blood alcohol content was twice the legal limit."

"Did you know about him?"

"You mean did I know about them."

She nodded.

"Yes. I knew about them."

She'd thought that grief had kept him vague, but now she could see a coldness in his eyes, something that Iola conjured in him. "Where was the cliff?"

"The cliff?"

"The one that they drove off."

He was about to respond but then stopped himself.

"Was it in France?" she asked. She wondered where the thought had come from. "Was it around here?"

He seemed all of a sudden concerned. She wondered if he would get prickly, which he sometimes did when she asked too many questions, but he just looked sad. She lowered her voice comically and said, "You can't keep anything from me, Carl." She put her hand on his. "I know everything." Although she didn't and would ask him more about it later.

To lighten the mood, she told Carl about the woman on the path, about how they were the first tenants in a long time. "Or at least that's what I think she said." And then as lightening things was creating its own strain, she said, "You brought me here because you want to like Mougins and your history was making it difficult and you thought by bringing me here, you would get it back."

"Get it back?"

"Make Mougins yours again."

He considered. "Yes," he said.

Whether or not this was true, it was a useful narrative. And he probably didn't know why he'd needed to bring her here, so why push him on it?

Carl had had more to drink and she offered to drive. She was accustomed to driving on this side of the road and the fact that she liked to drive—women in his world always let the men drive—amused him. Although the villa was not far from the village, there were a few complicated directional moves including an excessively signed roundabout, which offered many suggestions, none of which applied to where they were going. On the third circuit she took a guess at an exit, which proved to be right, and soon they were in the narrow tunnel with its odd glittering flag decoration (was it more bad art?) and then coming up to the Hotel Les Liserons that marked the turn for the road that zigzagged its way to the villa.

"I am just so happy with you," Carl said. He punched a button to put on the radio and found a station that was playing French techno music, which most often he detested. She realized he was quite drunk.

"Weren't you happy with Iola?" she asked, keeping the delivery light.

"Iola was magnificent, in a way that a horse is magnificent. But you don't want to live with a horse, and I quickly realized that I didn't want to live with her. I was going to divorce her, but she was making it difficult. She really didn't want me to be happy, and then she died." He was thinking things through. "I actually think you would have liked Iola. Not many women did. They found her intimidating, but you wouldn't have had a problem with her. She was exciting."

"Am I boring?"

"Yes," he said. "An absolute snore. I'm the luckiest man alive."

She looked quickly over at him, at his confused, contented face, and then—

There was a woman standing in the middle of the road. Yes. They were speeding and they would hit her. She slammed on the brakes and was turning the wheel hard to the left when Carl, suddenly alert, grabbed the wheel and held it straight. The car came to a stop and for several seconds neither said a word nor moved.

"We must have hit her."

"Hit who?" asked Carl.

"The woman. There was a woman. I was trying to avoid her—"

"You nearly went off the edge," said Carl.

Her door was already open and she took her phone, sending its beam around the road and into the steep drop into the valley. "Where is she?"

Carl had exited the car and was also looking. "I didn't see anyone," he said. The car was making bonging sounds as the doors were open and the key still in the ignition.

"I'm sure I saw her."

"You shouldn't have been driving," said Carl, more guilty than accusing.

"There was a woman. I am not drunk."

Carl looked her and nodded. "Maybe she wandered off."

"I—" She stopped.

"What?"

"I think I drove straight through her. I think I did." Carl pulled her into a hug and she stood there, her eyes wide. She was shaking.

* * *

Carl was on the phone when the owner dropped by. This time it was the wife who, thank God, spoke good English. The pool filter had stopped working, apparently clogged with leaves. The woman was bearing a bowl of figs and she set this on the kitchen counter.

"I apologize very much," said the woman. "Our caretaker left a few months ago. He had worked for us for years and then one day, he just goes. We are still looking for someone but now it is just my husband who takes care of this, and he is sometimes too busy." The woman looked around the house—it seemed nervously. "You like the house?"

"Yes," she said. "Very much. But the TV keeps coming on at two a.m. It does it every night."

"Ah," said the woman. She looked at the television and then, it seemed, up the hallway but quickly composed herself. "That is for the engineer. I will make a call."

But they were leaving in two days, so it didn't seem that the issue would be fixed before then.

Carl, done with his phone call, came down the winding stair. "Where is she?" he asked.

"The owner? Out unclogging the filter. We should remember to scoop the leaves." They watched through the living room window as the woman unlocked the maintenance chamber, which was on a level directly below the pool area. "How was your call?"

"Everything looks good. It appears that he is ready to sell the drawing." The drawing in question was a Picasso, genuine, that had been acquired seventy years ago by the seller's father. Apparently, the family had been friends of Picasso in his years in Mougins. The provenance of the artwork was unassailable. "So there's a dinner tonight in Nice. We should leave at seven."

"Oh God, Carl, don't make me go."

"Why not? It will be fun. The Paternaudes are lovely. And they have a fabulous wine cellar."

"Well, I think in spite of the fabulous wine cellar, I'd rather skip this one. They don't speak any English."

"She speaks some."

"Even worse. You'll be talking art and history and politics with the husband, and she'll be stuck talking to your American child bride about the weather and what I've done in Mougins. And the weather here doesn't change. And I haven't done anything."

Carl must have been relieved but was careful not to show it. "It might go late. I know I'm not the only agent who's seen the piece."

"Your charm is always more persuasive after midnight," she said, "and after some wine. But don't drink too much and don't speed. I'm still freaked out about last night."

They drove into Cannes for lunch and passed a few hours shopping. She tried on sunglasses but refused to buy any as they were too expensive and she already had a pair of Ray-Bans that she liked. In a café, where he had an espresso and she an Aperol spritz, she thought she recognized a young woman sitting at another table. The woman kept pawing at her hair with her hands flattened, moving the tresses without messing them up. Her hair was straight and heavily sprayed and this action—touching one's hair without actually affecting any change—seemed the sort of thing that famous people did. The woman must have been a celebrity, but she had no idea who it was. And Carl, of course, didn't know who it could be, although he thought that she should. Didn't young people know celebrities?

She thought she might nod off on the drive home. She was thinking about Iola, wondering what Iola would have thought of her. Would Iola have been pleased that Carl had ended up with an inferior, uncultured, ridiculous American? Would she have been offended that—given a second chance to choose—Carl had valued youth and good humor over her aristocratic sophistication? She looked over at Carl, who was navigating yet another roundabout with marked concentration. Maybe she would ask him later. Or maybe, after the effects of heat and Aperol had worn off, she'd think better of it. Carl would just try to humor her by saying assuring things, and this would make her feel stupid and like arguing that bland assurances weren't what she wanted. But if she didn't want that, what did she want? Then he'd say that it didn't matter. And he'd be right.

"Sleepy?" he asked.

"Absolutely," she said. "Let's take a siesta when we get home."

As they made the turns that led to the villa, she was thinking of the previous night. There had been a woman standing there. She was sure of it. Or was she? Because in the light of day the twisting road seemed unremarkable, just an ascent kept crumbling enough to discourage just anyone from driving up, a road that looked like it led nowhere and through nothing much.

Carl was showered and dressing and she was lying on the bed staring at the ceiling. "Don't wear a white shirt and don't wear a tie," she said.

"Why not?" he asked. She sat up and he was holding a white shirt, which looked perfectly acceptable. "Because you're not going to a funeral. Wear the pink. These are French people. And if another agent has been to see them, he was likely wearing a white shirt and a tie. Be different. Be the kind of man who knows billionaires."

"Billionaires trust people in white shirts and ties."

"Oh, whatever. What do I know?" she said. She collapsed back on the bed.

He went with the white shirt but left the tie in the closet.

"What will you have for dinner?" he asked, collecting his wallet and phone, putting them in his jacket pockets.

"Ham. Raspberries. Cheese."

"You look worried," he said.

"It's the TV. Do you think you'll be back by two?"

"I certainly hope so," he said.

On her Kindle she had downloaded *Thus Spoke Zarathustra* but found it unlikely that she would read it in time for them to go to Éze, and if she didn't read it for that purpose, why would she ever read it? No. She would keep going with her Sally Rooney novel. And there was always Netflix on his laptop. She would not touch the television.

"Are you really worried about the TV?" Carl said as he was leaving.

"I'll be fine." But she was worried.

"I've got an idea," he said. He walked into the living room and traced the network of cords to the appropriate wall plug. He pulled the plug from the wall, looked cursorily at it, and set it on the floor. "Why didn't we think of this earlier?"

"Try turning it on."

"It's unplugged."

"Just do it."

Carl picked up the remote and pressed the power button. Nothing happened. He smiled and set the remote down on the coffee table. "Happy?"

"So very heh-py," she said, imitating a mid-Atlantic, thirties movie accent.

*   *   *

She had fallen asleep with her novel, which was lying across her chest spread to the abandoned page. She was still wearing her reading glasses. She was alone in bed. Carl was in Nice with the Paternaudes. Why was she awake? Ah, her phone had pinged. She read the text. *Went late. Sorry! Leaving now.* It was one thirty in the morning. Weren't the Paternaudes old? But maybe there were young Paternaudes as well. All kinds of Paternaudes. Thin. Fat. Old. Young. Garrulous. Dull. She would no doubt hear all about it. She picked up her book, finding her place. She'd stay up to hear about the dinner. Carl wouldn't expect her to, but he would be pleased.

Precisely thirty minutes later, she heard the television come on. It was 2:00 a.m. At first she was annoyed, but then she remembered that Carl had unplugged it. Her mind began to race. Was it possible that the owners had come while she slept, had seen the plug lying on the floor and set it back in place? When would Carl be back? She sat listening to the sounds coming from downstairs—was it a talk show? The volume was, as always, very loud. She got up from the bed and put on Carl's robe. Despite the sound of the television, the house felt very still. She stood at the top of the winding stair, listening to the dialogue. Someone made a joke and someone else was laughing along with the sound of canned audience laughter. She was dizzy with fear but found herself taking careful steps downstairs. Yes. The television was definitely on. She stayed on the lowest rung of stairs, watching the show, a talk show, with a heavily made-up woman flirting with some young actor. And then, as if the chan-nel had changed, she found herself watching a dark road at night. The weirdness of it was riveting and she couldn't find the strength to go back upstairs and close the door, although she felt that was what she should do. There was something familiar about the road and the shot was tracking as if someone were walking down it, along the road, in the almost impenetrable darkness. Could it be the road to the villa? Yes she thought. It was. Someone was filming the road below the gate, approaching the first turn. A gentle wind was rustling the leaves, then the sound of a car engine could be heard, coming closer and closer. Someone was driving up the road and from the sound of it, driving quickly. The darkness began to brighten and then flash with headlights as the car, speeding, rounded the next bend. Then the car was barrel-ing straight into the shot. There was just a moment when she saw the driver. He hit the brakes, turned hard to the left, and then skidded off the road. He had crashed. There was a dull thunking of metal and the smashing of glass as the car bounced downward. And then the screen was dark. Before she had a chance to understand what she had seen, the channel switched again. There was the talk show, all garish color and braying laughter at an assaulting volume.

She had seen the driver of the car. The driver was Carl.

She stepped toward the coffee table, reaching for the remote, but the remote smoothly slid off the table and fell to the floor, thudding on the carpet. The remote had moved on its own. She remembered that the TV was unplugged and looked, and there was the plug, lying on the floor. The show was still playing. Also, she knew that she was being watched. The room had gone cold. She peered into the hallway and there was the shadow, thick as a person. As she watched, the figure turned and stepped to the kitchen wall and then through it.

She had to get out. She had to reach Carl. The house keys were hanging on the hook by the door. *A shadow cannot hurt you*, she thought. She willed herself to move and made quick steps through an eerie patch of deeper chill in the hallway and grabbed the keys. Then she was unlocking the door and the first gate. And then the second gate. She was running in her bare feet down the drive, past the carport. Was she being followed? She couldn't bear to look. And then she remembered that Carl had the remote for gate. How could she get out? It was a metal gate flanked by a stone wall. Could she climb over? Maybe, but it would be hard without shoes. And how would she reach the top of the wall? As her eyes adjusted to the dark, she made out a crate by the gatehouse. She moved the crate to the base of the wall and stepped onto it, holding to the wall for balance. As she pushed off from it, the crate wobbled and fell, but she pulled herself up with the strength of her arms. She swung a leg over the narrow wall and, for a heartbeat, lost her balance but managed somehow to recover. A surge of energy made her both alert and ill. The top of her left foot was stinging where she had scraped it on the way up, but she had made it. Her heart was pounding in her ears and she was dizzy with adrenaline. And then she was dropping down into a pile of leaves on the other side, scraped by branches. Carl's robe caught on some spike or thorn and she pulled it, ripping the fabric. Now she was free. Now she had to make it to the bottom of the drive as fast as she could. She looked back at the house and all the lights were blazing, although the only light she had left on was the one in the bedroom. Backlit, standing on the terrace, she thought she could see the figure, and even if her eyes were playing tricks, she felt for sure that someone was there, watching her. The moon was nearly full, lighting up the gravel on the path. She began to jog down, her ears alert to the sounds of rustling brush, of the breeze teasing the fine branches of the trees, rattling the leaves in the cool air. *Run*, she told herself. *Make it to the final bend. Stop Carl before he reaches that last turn.* And then she heard the car. He was coming. He would find her. She was screaming his name, running toward the light.

She had reached the corner and Carl would see her before he made the final turn. He was so near that she could hear the tires slipping on the gravel. French disco music pounded from the open windows of the car as the vehicle rounded the next bend. Now the drive was lit by the beams of the car. She thought she heard a laugh—a woman's laugh—but where had it come from? Who owned that laugh? It was a warning and suddenly her mind was flooded with sickening clarity. The headlights flared before her and she saw Carl's dread-stricken face, heard the panicked grit-spitting of tires on the graveled concrete as the car cut hard to the left and the world collapsed into an even darkness.

Vanishing Point

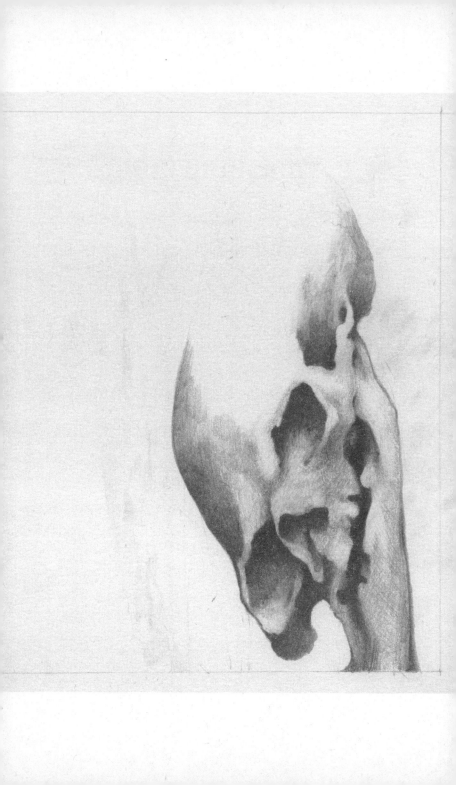

E ven in the eyes—no, especially in the eyes—one had to contend with the vanishing point. Eyes were spheres, not almond shaped, and behaved as spheres do, reacting to light and angle. Noses presented problems of their own, and cheekbones, and facial planes, but mastering the eyes was the hardest. Good eyes made a drawing come alive. His teacher had watched him struggle, had quoted Sargent, had said that "a portrait was a picture where something was wrong with the eyes." But Mark was going to get these eyes right, although he had to be patient. Right now, his skill was in leaving them as spheres, softly shaded, with no detail. Detail went in last. He was not a cartoonist, like Botticelli, with his hard lines and elegant details. He was Leonardo, working on the sfumato, the figures emerging from the soft matter of life.

"Always drawing," said his father, "even on a glorious day like this. You could at least attempt some plein air thing."

The rental on the Cape was ostensibly to create some time for Mark to enjoy his childhood before being shipped off again to the man factory that was Andover, for his mother to indulge in the final act of fawning motherhood as the summer ground to a close. As for his father—in his surgery during the week and only showing up on the weekends—it was an opportunity to entertain other city folk while rattling ice cubes in an endless progression of chunky cocktail glasses, although his father was careful with his drinking.

The house was on the edge of town, two blocks from the beach. It didn't have the wide porches of other vacation homes, like the one they'd rented the previous two summers, but seemed more of a regular house built for the sort of regular people who might have lived in it a hundred years earlier. There were three floors and two sets of staircases. The smaller one led directly to the kitchen, a reminder of servants shuttling up and down with stealthy industry. Although Mark could supply the original inhabitants—Edwardian men in wing chairs shaking out ironed newspapers, women wrapped in constricting silk and whalebone—the house seemed willfully empty of life, as if his imaginings were more real than he himself sitting on the scratchy fabric of the recliner in the living room or perched on the slightly small dining chairs as he sat to draw. The light in the dining room at this time of day was good, although in the evenings, the chandelier produced a smoky, diffused light that hearkened back to the time of gasoliers, as the bulbs—pretending to candles—weakly argued with the darkness.

His father had departed to the kitchen where his mother was drinking her coffee. Mark liked this house, its gloom, the smell of wood polish. There was a sadness about the place that his mother had attributed to its not having been let for several years. She thought no children had lived there, but she had no reason for this conclusion, just a hunch, and she trafficked in hunches.

A knock on the door and a cheery "hello" as it swung open announced the woman from the town who came in every morning and swept, replaced towels, made beds. She had curly red hair and a slim body and looked far too glamorous to actually be who she was.

"Hello, Mrs. Flintlock," said Mark. He closed his sketch pad.

"It's going to be hot today," she said.

As Mrs. Flintlock crashed around upstairs with the broom, Mark perused the books on the shelf in the study. Whoever owned the house previously had been a devotee of Southern Renaissance painting, and the shelves were packed with gloriously illustrated art books, the work of Ghirlandaio and Giorgione, Tintoretto and of course Leonardo—sketches, paintings, catalogs from exhibits mostly dating from the twenties, a collection that alluded to the wealth and taste of the former inhabitants of the house. Mark reached for a book on Uccello. The book, like all the others, was in near perfect condition. Mark held the covers loosely in his hands and let it drop open. Whoever had assembled this library had favorite works in all the books and this book fell to an image that must have been one of this number. It was *The Hunt in the Forest* and Mark felt struck by an odd affinity for the work. The piece was wide slung and done in jewel colors—blood reds, rich blues. There were hunters and horses and dogs, and they were all angled toward the center, as if enacting the lines of perspective clearly. Pillars of trees in the foreground and then smaller trees marked off clear lines of depth. A coy moon hovered behind the ranks, filtered through leaves. His eyes wandered through the painting. Something was off with perspective. For a painting so clearly conceived with planes of vision in mind, where was the vanishing point? At first it seemed near the center but then off to the left—and then right. Could the vanishing point be shifting? It drew the viewer in and then around, as a hunt might. Mark wondered why he was so drawn to it, as the figures—rocking horses, repeated dogs—seemed cartoonish and more representative of the medieval end of the Renaissance than the mannerist, but there was a flicker of memory in there, a flicker like that sliver of moon.

"Oh, that's pretty, isn't it?" his mother said, looking over his shoulder.

"Yeah. Sure." Mark was about to slam the book shut when a memory suddenly surfaced. "You showed me this," he said. "I remember us standing in front of it." He checked the location of the painting. "The Ashmolean. That's in Oxford. I remember you explaining it to me. You said something about me getting lost in it, to go as far as I could through the trees."

"Really?" said his mother. "How could you remember that? You must have been four years old when you were last in Oxford."

"Don't you remember?" he asked. "You remember everything."

"I remember what everyone ordered at every restaurant. That's not everything."

He wandered back into the living room. He could read or go for a walk. It was 10:00 a.m. He had to do something or else his father would get involved and he'd find himself fishing or at Colin Parker's house, whom he did go to school with but didn't like.

"It's too hot to garden," said his mother from the kitchen.

"Nonsense," said Mrs. Flintlock. "And it has to get done. Tomorrow the forecast is for rain, and Alice likes doing it. Although she did have a run-in with some poison ivy last week."

Mark could hear rustling around in the hydrangea outside. He went to the porch, letting the door slam behind him. There was a girl, roughly his age, a scarf around her head, pulling weeds from the bed.

"Hi," said Mark.

"You're Mark," she said, unimpressed, and went back to weeding. "My mother wants me to be friendly."

"You don't have to be," said Mark. "I'm not."

She tilted her face to him and smiled. She had blue eyes and her mother's skin. Her nose was peeling.

"I could give you a hand."

"Please don't. I get paid by the hour and I'm already weeding as slowly as I can."

He went back into the house. In the kitchen his mother was saying, "How could he remember that? He was just a baby."

And his father's reply. "He wasn't exactly a baby then, and more importantly he's not a baby now. Imagine if he was really—"

Then his mother saw Mark standing in the doorway. She silenced his father with a raised hand.

He had decided to go for a walk not because he wanted to walk but rather because he didn't want to be witnessed doing nothing. The weeding girl felt like a judgment. He paused on the porch steps wondering if he could pass her in silence but decided that would be a statement—that an actual statement would be less of a statement.

"See you later," he said.

Alice looked up and raised a neutral hand.

The town quickly exhausted itself and Mark soon found himself on the beach. He wasn't wearing trunks as he wasn't much of a swimmer and found little to enjoy in wading through pebbles and seaweed in order to tread water in the cold, green chop. He was thinking about his drawing, a woman's face, angled and looking up and to the left. He wasn't sure where the inspiration was coming from. Although there was nothing in the painting that would allow him to explore the sfumato effects and deep shadow that playing with this unknown woman's portrait did. He watched the shadow of a seagull track quickly across the sand and in following it came dangerously close to walking over a sandcastle. He looked up and saw a child watching him, spade in hand, judging. The way the child looked at him made him feel more of the world of adults than of children.

After dinner, Mark went up to his room. His parents were still working on a bottle of wine in the dining room and he could hear his mother laughing at some story she had no doubt heard a dozen times before. His roommate's parents had divorced last year, and he had heard all about their fights, their silences, the endless division of houses and friends and even the dog. Something about that clear enactment of family misery had appealed to him because his own sense of unease about his parents was unjustified. He had a hale and hearty dad, who had been a lacrosse player and was now a doctor but didn't demand the same of his son and seldom lost his temper. And he had Mimi, his mother, who looked at everything he did with a sort of supportive wonder. But still there was a sense of his being unsettled. His mind wandered back to *The Hunt in the Forest* and he considered the image, tracking some unknown thing between the trunks of the trees. When his parents finally went to bed, it was nearly midnight. His book was uninteresting, a mystery pulled off the shelf in the bedroom, a book with grains of sand in the pages. He went downstairs and took a cigarette from his mother's pack on the shelf and went to the yard, closing the door silently behind him. He really didn't like smoking that much, but the act of it felt good. Most of the boys smoked at school and it was one way not to stand out. The moon was nearly full and the yard bright, stretching in a flat, uninterrupted plane to the wall of trees. He took a shallow drag and sent a stream of smoke into the night air, which dissipated in a forking series of rivulets, bending in the light breeze. He had a moment's paranoia. Was he being witnessed? The lamp in his parents' room was off, but there was a soft glow inside, probably light drifting in from the hall, and had someone been watching at the window, he would have been able to see them. There was no one there. But still, he couldn't shake the feeling. A quiet descended—a heavier stillness—until his heavy breathing, sawing in and out, seemed the only thing arguing against the silence. And then he saw her, a woman, standing at the perimeter of trees. She was wearing a nightdress—long, white—but her ankles and bare feet were still visible. She was at such a distance that he couldn't make out her face, but the two stood in silent observation of each other. She raised a hand to him, stretching it out, and took a step forward. Mark watched, unable to move, but then, as if in a dream, she seemed to disappear or to retreat back into the forest. Which had it been? There was a strange disconnect between what he saw and how his mind had processed it. It wasn't until she disappeared from view that Mark felt certain he had not been meant to see her, that something strange had put her at the edge of the woods, that he had somehow drawn her forth.

Mark set himself up leaning against the house beneath the kitchen window, shaded by a vigorous hydrangea that was being menaced by thrumming bees. He would draw the wall of woods and perhaps that figure, with her hand raised, but after attempting the trees, the flatness was discouraging. His usual skill at perspective was given no challenge, and he found himself returning to the portrait of the woman with her head angled like a saint. Slowly her cheekbones were emerging from the shadow, her eyes gently tilting upward. From inside, he could hear the ceramic clunking of morning coffee cups, the heavy tread of his father entering the kitchen. Mimi sighing by an open refrigerator door.

"Do memories come back?" she asked.

"You're thinking of Mark. He was only four. He won't remember her."

And then the refrigerator slammed shut.

"Marie, you're all the mother he needs."

Mark watched Mimi swim out to the buoy. She liked to keep her hair out of the water, which made her progress slow. Mimi's name was actually Marie. That he should baby talk "Mommy" into "Mimi" made sense, but he could also have done so with Marie. Mimi was young to be his mother—twenty-one when he was born, a solid ten years younger than his father. Mimi was blond and Mark had always been convinced—in a feat of cognitive separation—that his mother was actually the dark-haired woman in his dreams, the woman always pointing at something that he could not make out.

She came up the beach and he tossed her a towel. He said, "Mimi, why have we never gone back to Oxford? We went there all the time when I was little."

"Oxford is boring. I like London much better. That's why we go there."

"There are no pictures of the Oxford trips, no pictures from when I was little."

"Yes there are."

"There's the one of me and Dad by the building with all the heads."

"There must be some others. I probably have my eyes closed in all of them." Mimi forced a laugh. "Aren't you going in?"

Wednesday was the day that Alice mowed the lawn. Mark awoke to hearing the even back-and-forth of shear-ing grass. He looked out the window, and there she was, bandanna on her head, pushing then dragging the mower. She looked up at the house and caught him at the window and waved.

Mark dressed quickly and went downstairs. Mimi was stirring a pitcher of lemonade. Her feet were bare and she was humming to herself.

"Mother?" said Mark. He assessed this woman.

"How can you already be in a mood? You're barely awake. Here." She poured a glass of lemonade. "Take this out to Alice."

Alice had stopped mowing to watch Mark walk across the lawn with the glass. He thought she might meet him halfway, but she didn't, just wiped her hands on her grass-stained shorts. She didn't thank him.

"I'll be done mowing lawns at three," she said. "We could go to the movies."

"All right."

Alice nodded. "But you have to pay. I'm saving up for a car."

"How old are you?"

"Fifteen." She looked at the remaining spread of nodding, untamed grass. "Cars are expensive."

Mark worked on his drawing in the afternoon and then, because it was something he had to do, cracked open his math book. He didn't want to have to take advanced algebra and if he could just test out of it, that would be one less math class for next year. A page of foolscap was marred with faulty equations that he'd abandoned and now a loose pencil drawing of the woman he'd seen at the edge of the woods—her long black hair, her raised hand.

"Alice is here," called Mimi. She looked very pleased.

Mark nodded to Alice and headed down the steps. They walked past the first few houses in silence.

"Your mother's nice," said Alice.

"She's not my mother."

"Who is she?"

"I think she's the au pair. That's the only way it makes sense."

"The only way what makes sense?"

"That I've known her all my life, that it would be possible to replace my mother and think that time would erase my memory of her."

"What happened to your mother?"

"I'm guessing she died somehow." Mark thought of the woman at the edge of the woods, of her raised hand. "Maybe she killed herself."

They sat in the back seat of the movie theater watching as a creature slid out of the primordial ooze. A woman ran screaming. Mark turned to kiss Alice, but she pushed him off. "This is the best part."

"You've seen this before?"

"Twice." Alice watched the screen as she undid the top button of her shirt. "But don't worry. It's the only bit worth watching."

After the credits were rolling, Mark and Alice exited the theater. It was still bright out and the tables at the clam shack were filling with patrons. "Let's go to the beach," said Alice.

They walked along the packed sand. Mark had his hands in his pockets and Alice looked over at him every now and then, assured by the silence.

"Do you believe in ghosts?" asked Mark.

"No."

"You sound certain."

Alice shrugged. "That house you're staying in is supposed to be haunted, but before you showed up, me and some of my friends got in through a window and spent the night. And there was nothing. We were really quiet. We had a Ouija board. And then Susan's mother called my mother because she'd forgotten her inhaler. And they figured out what we were doing and we got in trouble. All for bullshit."

"Maybe I brought the ghost."

"Did you see a ghost?"

"I might have. I saw a woman in the backyard last night. She didn't seem real."

Alice looked him up and down. "You're kind of weird. Are rich people always fucked up?"

Mark gave it a moment's thought. "In my experience, yes."

*   *   *

On Saturday, Mimi persuaded Mark's father that it would be fun to have the Flintlocks over for dinner. Mr. Flintlock—Frank—worked as a contractor but usually had a house that he was fixing up for resale. "Does he follow sports?"

"Red Sox, I'm afraid."

"I will try to avoid fisticuffs."

Mark was working on his drawing, and it was nearly done. He felt with certainty that he had drawn his mother, that locked in his memory her image was still intact, and that he'd managed her likeness. He thought of the woman standing at the edge of the woods. He remembered the way she had raised her hand, as if she wished she could touch him. He felt certain she was his mother and hoped she would return.

The Flintlocks arrived shortly after six. Mark's father was charming Mrs. Flintlock, who, flattered, was responding with a slightly hysterical good humor. Mr. Flintlock had tried to engage Mark on sports, and Mimi's rescue—"Mark is really into art"—had met with the usual awkward attempts at interest.

"I think it's wonderful," said Mrs. Flintlock, in reference to some wonderful thing. "Alice is saving up for college."

Alice and Mark exchanged a look. And then they cleared the plates.

Alice said, "We're going for a walk."

Alice and Mark walked side by side and Mark took her hand. He held it for a while, but then it felt heavy and as if it wasn't really a part of her, so he let it go.

"You think I'm weird," he said.

"I like you," she responded. They stopped to kiss and then continued walking along the edge of the woods. She was telling him about a football game at her school and how this one girl had had too much to drink and the other kids talked about her and then she had to drop out of school.

"What did she do?" asked Mark.

"She didn't do anything. It's what the guys did. And they're still there. It's not fair."

He felt somehow responsible. He didn't even know the girl's name.

"Don't be sad," said Alice. "She's okay. She's working at the Seven-Eleven."

And then he saw the woman—or he thought he did. A flash of white that moved slowly into the trees and out of sight.

"Did you see that?"

"I thought I might have . . . I don't know. Is there someone out there?"

"Yeah. I think there is." He picked up his pace, but Alice had dropped behind. "We're going to lose her."

"Her?"

"I think it's her. Don't chicken out on me."

Alice sighed audibly and then joined him, taking his hand. They picked a path between the trees and just when it seemed that there was no one, that they had somehow been mistaken together, they saw her. It was definitely a woman, although too far away in the moonlight to see her features. Something in her manner seemed incredibly sad. She raised her hand, and although her gesture was not pointing, she seemed to be gesturing at Mark. Alice let go of Mark's hand and stepped back. "Mark," she whispered.

"Don't worry," Mark said. "She just wants to see me."

"We should go." Alice didn't know how she found those words or how she turned and ran, but the next sound that was clear to her was that of her legs crashing through a tangle of undergrowth and her own breath tearing at her lungs.

"Well, they seem to be getting along," said Mrs. Flintlock. She was on her third gin and tonic.

Mimi kicked her shoes off and rested her bare feet on the edge of her husband's chair. "They are getting along, which is great, because if they weren't, Mark would spend all of his time drawing. And if he's going to do that, why not just stay in the city all summer? And this is such a great house. Are we really the first people to stay in it?"

"Oh, yeah," said Mr. Flintlock. "I had to redo all the wiring before the owners could let anyone in, and that took a while. And there was an issue with the upstairs bathroom. Until this summer, the house had just been empty."

"Why would the owners allow that?" asked Mark's father. "This is prime real estate. Couldn't they sell it?"

"There was some problem with the inheritance. And the house has quite a history."

"Is it a good story?" asked Mimi.

"Frank, don't," said Mrs. Flintlock. "They're going to think all the townspeople are superstitious and ignorant."

"And they'd be right," said Mr. Flintlock. "If you grow up here, you know the story. The Deering family, who owned this house, had a tragedy, I think it was in eighteen eighties. Apparently, Mrs. Deering was at the beach with their two-year-old son, and she got distracted. The kid drowned."

"Oh, how horrible," said Mimi.

"That's not the end of it," said Mr. Flintlock. "They bury their child and go into mourning. Then Mrs. Deering is found in the woods in the back of the house and she's hanged herself."

"Wow," said Mark's father. "That is a story."

"Not done, Nate," said Mr. Flintlock. "Her family wants her death investigated because they think that Deering did her in. He blamed her for the kid's death, and the whole thing is investigated. You can read about it at the town library. They didn't have enough evidence to convict. But everyone thinks he did it."

"Why?" asked Mimi.

"Because no one could figure out how she'd gotten herself into the tree. There was a chair nearby, looking kicked out, but it didn't really line up. And, weird detail, she wasn't wearing any shoes and her feet were completely clean. It had rained the night before and she should have had mud on her or on the edge of the nightgown, but there was nothing. So everyone just thought that Deering had done it, strangled her or something like that, and then carried her body out and made it look like she'd hanged herself."

"Wouldn't he have had to put the body on the muddy ground while he set up the rope?" said Mark's father.

"Maybe he set it up first."

"He'd still have to put the body down and then haul it up—"

"Nate, please!" said Mimi.

"Maybe he had the body in a wheelbarrow. Heck if I know. I'm just telling you what the locals say. When we were kids, they were still saying that she'd show up and steal the children away. That she was a vengeful spirit."

"A vengeful spirit? Really, Frank," said Mimi.

"Oh, yeah," said Mr. Flintlock. "Vengeful. They said she used to lure kids out to the rock quarry. It's about a mile back there"—he gestured out the back door—"and they'd slip in the dark, get discovered the next day floating facedown in the water. It looked like an accident, but we knew it was Alma Deering."

Mrs. Flintlock laughed. "I'm laughing now, but when I was a kid, I was terrified." She had picked up Mark's sketchbook and was leafing through the drawings. She came to stop on the portrait of the woman. "Who is this?" she asked. "She's very striking."

"Wow," said Mark's dad. He got up from his chair, taking the sketchbook from Mrs. Flintlock. "It's Mark's mother. He hasn't seen her since he was four. How could he remember?"

"I didn't realize—" said Mrs. Flintlock, looking to Mimi, uncertain.

"Yes. But he doesn't know. He was so little that it just seemed easier to . . . I don't know. To let him think of me as his mother. I guess it was naive to think he'd never figure it out."

"That's understandable," said Mrs. Flintlock. "How did she die?"

"She didn't," said Mark's father. He laughed wryly. "She took off with a French artist and last I heard was living in Paris. I doubt she looks like this now." He dropped the sketchbook on the table. "I need another drink. Any takers?"

First Cause

First Cause

E vening was fading to night and the light showed sharper, first around his shoulders, then over the features of his face—the sloping brow, the hollowed sockets, the sharp cheekbones and hard-set mouth. She was aware of the space between them and then of the bitter glint of his eyes, which he was slowly raising to meet her own. Toby said nothing at first, just inspected her across the expanse of table, a frigid scape of dusted maple that was impossible to breach.

"What do we talk of tonight?" he said finally, his voice faintly echoing.

"What is left?"

A low chuckle escaped his pale lips. "For me, nothing. For you—"

"Whatever you have left me." And what had he left her? A sense of yearning and the unfinished, a sense that they would never be done. If she had been more confident, she would have been able to push back, to make him see her fully. But she had failed in that and now was confronted with him before her, and while he ought to have been just a reminder of her marriage, of her partnership with this man, he was not, but more her awareness of all that was impossible between them. Could he hear her thoughts? It was impossible to know. "If only I wasn't so alone. Then maybe I wouldn't be losing my mind."

"Ah. So we are back there," he said. "You were always one never to let go of a thing but to pretend you had."

"And you were always one to dodge what I was trying to talk about by pointing out some shortcoming on my part." Toby's face was somehow underlit, the shadows weak, but she could sense a tightening of his mouth. "Why did we do what you wanted to do?" she asked.

"We did nothing of the sort. What we did was maintain the status quo, which was to have no child. To have a child would have been an action. You would have had to argue for the change, to show that this action would positively impact our lives. And in that you failed. You were unable to prove how having a child would have made things better. You would always fall to some weak appeal to what normal people did, without being able to define 'normal' or being able to adequately illustrate the value of 'normalcy,' even if you had been able to do it."

"Ten years with you made me a stranger to the normal. How could I define it? Everyone I thought was normal was doing something that I wasn't allowed to do."

"And you think that having a child would somehow have saved you? You don't know that. You don't know how the future would have played out. A child could have complicated things further. What if you were inadequate to the necessary tasks of motherhood? What if it had fallen ill?"

"What if he or she hadn't?"

"You will get nowhere arguing like that. The possibility of making an accurate assessment based on an uncertain future is—"

"Is impossible. I get it." Elia placed her hands catlike on the table. What if she had reached out and touched him? What then? "But what about giving me something that I wanted, because that would be a good thing to do for a person that you loved. Maybe you could have done something just to see me happy."

Toby tilted his head. "And that might have been a good, and if it were a good, let's see how it balances out against other goods. My need to have peace in the house, surely that is a good. When it came to finances, we were barely making it. This additional person would have been a drain on that. And the world doesn't need more people." He was nodding now, pleased with the progression of thought. "Our staying childless was the more reasonable proposition."

"Okay." She mirrored his head tilt, a mockery. "But if you break it apart, it doesn't hold. We were spending money on things that could have helped toward the household expenses."

"You mean that I was spending money on things that could have helped toward household expenses."

"I always supported you in your work, but can't you see that maybe all of the purchases weren't necessary?"

"You're talking about the Heidegger."

Elia steeled herself. "It was a first edition."

"It was not the object but what I brought to it, what it signified."

"It was over two thousand dollars." Elia watched the light shift across his face, an illusion of shadow on the table. "It was in German."

"I read German."

"Not as well as English. If it had helped you in your understanding or helped you finish your book, I would have understood that. But any book in English would have helped you more."

"You can't prove that."

"But you did buy the book, and since you did it, and that's what's real, don't you have to prove that it helped you?"

"What are you talking about?"

"Like the existence of God. You have to prove that he exists. You can't say that it's impossible to prove that he doesn't exist."

"What does a first edition *Sein und Zeit* have to do with the existence of God?" The mockery now had a sympathetic edge, as if she were a deluded child.

"It's the teapot," Elia said warily. "The one that's orbiting the earth."

"Russell's Teapot." Toby's head dipped, weighted with patience. "And?"

Elia had often wondered what it would have been like to be one of Toby's students, but they all loved him. "You have to prove that the teapot is orbiting the earth. It's not enough to say that you can't prove that the teapot isn't orbiting the earth." She felt certain that he saved this intolerance for her. "But that's not the point, is it?"

"There's a point?"

"Yes." The point was that Toby had needed to feel that he was a real philosopher and because the first edition Heidegger was something that he felt a real philosopher would own, he had achieved his goal. His dissertation supervisor, who Toby felt had never taken him seriously, had coveted a first edition *Sein und Zeit*, and when Toby had come across it on AbeBooks, he'd bought it without consulting Elia—an act of revenge against this retired professor, in case he, too, was trawling the site and might be able to fulfill his dream.

"And the point is?"

The point was that if Elia acknowledged this spiteful side to Toby, he would shift to rage. And no progress would be made. And they needed to progress, because she wanted the conversation to end, existed in that hope.

"You don't need to tell me. I know what you're thinking."

She knew that he did not but also that it didn't matter. That in their marriage, what he thought she was thinking was the narrative of merit, and so she waited for Toby to tell her what occupied her mind, as his creation of it would be the practical reality.

"You're thinking that if I'd finished my book, things would have been easier."

She was thinking it now. Yes, Toby would have had that approval, that pride, a book on the shelf to sit next to the first edition *Sein und Zeit* to validate his thought. He'd taken a year's leave without pay to finish the manuscript and she'd taken extra work as a tutor to make ends meet. The manuscript had gained mass without actually progressing. Yes, it would have been nice for Toby to be tenured instead of his having to renegotiate his tenure year as he wrangled with his publisher to extend the deadline, the specter of being recast as lecturer with greater teaching demands hovering. Although what was wrong with that? Toby was an excellent teacher. Didn't she know it. And yes, she had supported him, told him he could do it, all the while waiting for Toby's Copernican Revolution in semiotics to take the work of Wittgenstein and Lyotard and Derrida, this endless stream of men, to a place that had not yet been staked and claimed. And along with everyone else, Toby too, she had come to believe that he would never get there simply because he was too grounded in the thoughts of others—too believing in what they'd achieved—to think he would ever bring it further. If she'd ceased to believe in him, Toby's life would have been intolerable, so she maintained a position, avoiding the alternate even in argument with self. It was dishonesty masquerading as kindness. No. Dishonesty was kindness. In this moment, the two concepts occupied the same territory, were somehow the same thing, had more in common than less in common and were, therefore, in possession of enough common ground to be approaching the identical. "If things were easier, you would have finished your book."

When they first met, Toby had been a man alive with ideas—quick minded, full of promise. He was inarguably possessed of a fine intellect and anything he trained it on had lit up as a result of the attention. She too—a hard worker, a solid paper writer, a deadline maker—had come alive with his attention. She had found his rationality a tonic after a previous relationship, one where every argument came down to an appeal to emotion, her ex's gaping passions so much greater than her own that she had felt invisible, even to herself. She had thought herself saved by Toby, had thought that through the supremeness of conscious dialogue that she was speaking her way into a more realized version of self. He had buoyed her, made her feel capable of things that before she had felt inadequate even to imagine. But as Toby's opportunities had slowly closed off and the objectives onto which his intellect had been drawn shown a limited promise, he focused increasingly on her. And as the subject of his study, her inadequacies had quickly mounted. She felt continuously exposed—or on the brink of exposure—an anxiety of being that she could only escape when in her classroom, asking her students to earnestly sympathize with an endless array of fictional characters, their beings held safely within book covers, easily explicated, discussed in the simplest of ways: quizzes sought to elicit responses about what characters had done to determine whether or not students had read books; essays assigned to determine whether or not they had understood what they'd read. She'd shored herself up with endless sheaves of work to correct, a stream of meetings and curriculum days—and then tutoring on the side—and felt that in these moments she knew who she was. To return to Toby's difficulties at the end of the day was to shelve her being in order to better understand his, as that was what the work in the marriage had become. Where was the man who had dominated every cocktail party, who could accurately attribute every concept, who had a font of ideas for papers and—one day—books, who was only challenged by the lack of time to put it down? How were this man and that man the same?

He was there at the end of the table, nothing but a shadow now, and the room looked cold; although she could not adequately sense whether this was the case.

"If you wish to say that if things were easier, I would have finished my book, you must define what these things are."

She felt her shoulders bow under the weight of this next task. "Sometimes," she said, "I don't know who you are. I can't. But I have a solid memory of who you were and have a hard time believing that the two are somehow the same."

"Ah," he said. "Let me explain this to you. Materialists would say that my occupying the same body implies that the *before* me and the *current* me are identical, but of course that has its problems. Is my body at the time of my being six years old the same body as that of mine now? Even the mass of the two bodies involved is different. Descartes states that the existence of a sameness of soul determines identity. But of course, that requires a belief in God, causality, all of that. So thank God"—here his voice dripped with irony—"for Kant and his Copernican Revolution, which gives us consciousness. Sameness of consciousness, a present self that has a memory shared with the past self, to give us who we are. We are our consciousness, body be damned. Soul"—more irony—"be damned." His face was distorted then, a wash of gray acting across his features. "I am of the opinion that I am very much the same person. I remember me. I remember you. I remember this marriage."

But his memory of the marriage was different from hers. He had thought her unbearably bourgeois and she had defined him by his dissatisfaction, always waiting to strike. Each termed the struggle "marriage," but as their struggles related to different things, the struggles could not be termed as identical, or shared. "We remember our marriage in different ways," she said.

"Of course. And there is a term that exists, 'marriage,' that we bandy about in conversation because how else does one discuss it, this different thing?"

"Wittgenstein's Beetle," she said. She remembered the beetle as a part of their courtship ritual, when she had thought semiotics more intriguing than horrifying. Wittgenstein had presented the idea that if a number of people were holding boxes and the thing in the boxes was a beetle, that they could talk about this "beetle," which would signify the thing in the box without ever coming to an agreement about what a beetle was. A beetle could have been a thimble or a hairpin or a mouse. Language, language, language. As a child, Elia had wondered if what she saw as red was what other children saw as red or if they thought it was blue. There was, apparently, an entire field of study that was devoted to this, that tied into physics, that was there to take the everyday and to torture it into something so complex and deranged as to make life fraught with inexplicable, limitless horror. "I have always tried to support you," she said.

"True," Toby responded. His face blurred momentarily, then came into focus. "But your work always came first."

He surprised her. Had he surprised her before? "How can you say that? I have always made decisions based on what was good for us."

"Elia, Elia, Elia." His figure wavered with each address. "So you say. But did you give it up for us or did you just give it up? Or just give up?"

She had been pursuing a PhD in English with a focus on the Edwardians. She was interested in writing about furniture, which might seem silly, but there was some significant furniture to be dealt with. Consider the bookcase in *Howards End*. But after meeting Toby, she had decided to pursue a master's with a certificate in teaching. She had abandoned the Edwardians and their furniture to teach *The*

Bean Trees to high school freshmen. Her decision to shift had been practical. A university would never have given both tenure. "I didn't give up," she said. "I made a decision that was good for both of us."

"By 'us' you mean the usual 'you.' You became a high school teacher for me."

"You are part of 'us,' so yes."

"And so you are saying that the decision was good for 'us.' How can that be if you consider that it was bad for you? How could it have been good for 'us' if a solid half of the parties involved were adversely affected?"

"I didn't say that I was adversely affected."

"But that is what you think."

"At the time, it was a sacrifice but not one that I regretted. I liked teaching in the high school. I liked my students."

"But you often wondered what it would have been like had you not made that decision, had you continued on."

"It's only human to think that way."

"And so you admit to that but not to having regrets?"

Why would she admit to regret? He was setting the trap for her, where she resented him and all the possibility that he had robbed from her, where that resentment was unfounded because she had no basis for concluding that the future would have been kinder. "You have already proven the futility of such thinking," she said. "It is Schrödinger's Cat."

"Ah," he said. "It is your 'Schrödinger's Cat.'"

"My Schrödinger's Cat?"

"Your Schrödinger's Cat, which you always use to illustrate the impossibility of reasoning using an unknown future as a factor, when the Cat actually means something of a different nature, that one exists in a state of not knowing whether the cat is alive or dead because the cat is in a box, and that, as it is not witnessed, the cat is actually existing in those two states. And Schrödinger argued this against the Copenhagen Interpretation that a quantum superposition can exist in multiple states until the process of witnessing causes it to collapse into a specific outcome. Schrödinger points out that this is problematic as it is not the process of witnessing that defines whether the cat is alive or dead."

"Then if I have been so wrong, why did you allow me to use that for so long?"

"Because I was accepting what it came to signify to you, and because we could discuss based on your understanding of it. Your use of it allowed us to further discussion. Your sense of the thing became useful, although in a limited way. It was part of our word game."

"Word game?" She was nearly sobbing. "But all I see is that I've never understood anything, never could, or if I did, it was useless in our solving our problems."

"That's not entirely true."

"So what is a truth about us that would satisfy you?"

"The truth is that if you had had a need to be satisfied, that would have satisfied me. Perhaps it is this that killed us." But he could see that he was losing her, that she was disappearing, her edges blurring and the wall behind her slowly becoming visible as she diminished.

"No, Toby. It was a gas leak that killed us. Carbon monoxide."

"There is hope for us," he said with urgency. "We are not all blood and bone."

"We are the cat," she said, "alive and dead and with no witness to tell us which it is."

"We are our consciousness. We are ourselves." But as he urged this, he, too, was feeling that thinness that ended all their conversations. "Don't go," he begged. "I cannot exist without you, without you to see me—"

The Third Boy

W ell, however long ago it was, it feels even longer. It was the year that your father was on sabbatical. One of his collaborators, affiliated with Saint Hilda's, had put together a grant to work on a Rameau opera, *Castor and Pollux*. It had long been your father's dream to do something like this as Rameau was out of favor in the US, if he'd ever been in favor, and no one seemed to care about the baroque. He found us a house—actually part of a refurbished barn—that he selected on account of its high ceilings and also because it came with a piano, and he moved us all to Oxfordshire. I was already five months pregnant, so I felt that I knew you in a way. At the time, I was still working as musical director at the Episcopal church on Newbury Street, which mostly involved playing harp at weddings and sometimes funerals and managing the choir as they reached for notes and descended into petty squabbles. I was happy to quit. And absolutely thrilled to spend the final months of my pregnancy unemployed and out of reach of my mother, who had already warned me that she thought I'd find motherhood "challenging," that she feared I wasn't a "natural mother."

The house was just outside of Oxford city proper in a town called Nuneham Courtenay. We were at the end of a paved lane off the Reading road. Close by was the ring road—torn along by screaming cars or stunned with traffic—and just beyond that the bustle of Headington, the cramped quaintness of Summertown, the chatter of Jericho, and the austere circus of the university itself, but where we were seemed straight out of Hardy: fields shocked to a Van Gogh yellow by blooming rapeseed, or stitched over with pink fritillaries, or somberly productive with the bobbing, knee-high wheat of late spring. The Thames was just beyond the fields and if you were standing on the rail fence that bordered our yard, you could just make out the shimmer of water, although the land dropped in such a way as to make it not quite clear. There were cows along the banks and one saw the cows and knew, at least, that the cows were seeing the river.

Our time in Oxford was one of my happiest. That's where you were born and *Castor and Pollux*—when it was finally rolled out—was a triumph. When it wasn't raining, I would sit with you on a blanket in the soft English sun reading novels. And even the rain seemed a benediction to me. I felt as shielded by it as the deer who showed up to nibble at the hedges. It was ideal. It was. And even now I wonder if the one afternoon that clouds it was but a shudder of the mind, a glitch, because it seemed so impossible. Although the disproving of it, ultimately, presented more impossibilities than its believing.

We'd been in the house just over a month, and I had taken to rambling around the fields. Sandford-on-Thames was a short walk across a meadow and if you headed south along the Thames you would reach Nuneham House, with its gardens and lawns and peacocks.

Across the river there was Radley College that announced itself with a daily regatta of rowing boys madly trying to outpace each other up and down the Thames. My regular path to the river started behind the garages into a stretch of woodland. Beneath a tree—some sort of beech as its great branches reached out close to the ground, elbowing the earth in spots—a sort of cave had been created by the low limbs, trunk, and leaves. In its shelter, someone had set a table and chairs—child-size. One of the chairs had a rabbit drawn on its back in chipping paint. I had not noticed any children in the nearby houses. The barn seemed to favor the older dons, ones whose sons and daughters had already headed to university. I wondered if the table and chairs, the setting for a mad little tea party, belonged to an earlier time or if I had yet to see the child or children responsible for its upkeep.

I was close to thirty and very nearly a mother, but something in the area awakened my imagination, a sense of wonder, and gave each natural thing—the sun, a rainbow, a rabbit sniffing the air—a weighted, gorgeous significance.

That afternoon I was tidying the kitchen, having let the breakfast dishes and my lunch plate pile up, when I looked out the window and saw a flash of color—a shock of blue. I ran through the living room to the other side of the house, where I imagined this blue had gone and there, stalking about the rail fence, was a peacock. I rushed outside in my bare feet and was quite delightedly following the thing when the wind picked up and a loud slam, which sent the peacock on its way, announced to me that I had locked myself out. The weather changed very quickly at that time of year and as I wasted a half hour jiggling at the locks and peering into the empty homes of my immediate neighbors while the wind—now gusting in fits—pulled at my hair, I began to think that I would spend the rest of that bleak afternoon cowering in the doorway. I hoped your father would come home at a reasonable hour. A handful of raindrops clattered across the footpath that led to the door.

I was in a thin shirt and getting cold, the rain already dampening my jeans and the discomfort of my situation dilating time in such a way that each minute was already taking forever, when I saw a woman cross the stile at the edge of the garden. She did not head across the front of the barn, which would have meant that she was the one neighbor I had yet to meet, but took the break between the hedges and proceeded down the single-lane road that led to the carriageway. The woman moved at a good clip, understandable as the rain was picking up and, although she was wearing a Barbour jacket, her head was bare. I hadn't yet wandered up that way because the fields were so appealing, as was the village, and this direction seemed to offer little if one were on foot. I might have called out, but I felt too ridiculous, so I just followed her to the little brick house set where the road curved to the left, a house hidden by a wall of greenery that I'd only passed in the car.

She was shielded by the hedge as she entered the house. When I reached the door, it was open a crack. I called into the dark hallway and, not having the sort of nerves that some do, was about to leave when she appeared suddenly beside me.

"Can I help you?" she asked.

"I'm afraid you can," I said. "I'm living at South Barn and I've locked myself out. Can I use your phone to call my husband?"

The woman was tall, blond, and possibly my age or a few years older. She had long-fingered, exquisite hands, what my husband called pianist hands. Her face was oval-shaped like a Modigliani and she tilted it, looking at me as she sighed. "I'm afraid my phone is out of service." I saw her eyes descending, first past my pregnant middle and then to my bare, wet feet.

"I saw a peacock." This was supposed to explain my appearance in her house.

"No doubt escaped from Nuneham House," she said. She sighed again, resigned. "If we sit in the kitchen, you'll be able to see when your husband returns."

"Or one of my neighbors. I hate to impose."

"On what?" she said. I followed her down the hall-way, mostly decorated with unimaginative prints of Oxford landmarks—Christ Church, the Sheldonian—excepting a portrait of my host in orange chalk on blue paper. She, who had yet to introduce herself, saw me looking at it and said, "My honeymoon. That was done in Montmartre."

This was when I should have introduced myself, but the moment passed, and she continued through the doorway. We sat in the kitchen on opposite sides of a small table. I could have used some tea, but she didn't offer any. The house was so silent that one understood how quiet and still could be synonyms, how timelessness projected itself without sound to mark progressing instants. Outside, the rain had found its force and was flogging itself against the panes in sheets of water. The obvious conversation points—who I was, why I was in Oxford—seemed not to interest her. I looked around the room as she watched the water coursing over the glass, her chin now resting delicately on the heel of her hand, her elbow planted on the back of another chair. There was a pinch pot set on the windowsill above the sink with a crude figure of a rabbit head drawn on it, and I wondered if she had children.

"When is your baby due?" she asked suddenly.

"September," I said. A moment passed. "My husband and I are very excited," I added, because that's what people say and I couldn't think of anything else.

"Children." She smiled. "This is a great area for children. You know that Lewis Carroll used to go boating up and down this stretch of Thames. It's true. The bit in *Alice in Wonderland* where she and the mouse are swimming in a pool of tears was written after he was caught in a rainstorm this side of Sandford Lock."

"I hadn't heard. How interesting."

"Not far from here they found the remains of a Roman kiln. The Pitt Rivers is full of stuff they've dug up around here, as is the Ashmolean. They have a small statue of Diana. So, Roman gods, but there are also the barrows of the Celts and whatever is preserved in muck lying just beneath the surface, either waiting to be dug up or hoping that time will slowly erase all memory of it, all need for it, all interest. At Nuneham House, they still believe in the old Celtic ways."

"Really? I thought it was owned by the university."

"Yes. And leased. Perhaps the university doesn't know what the house is used for. Once, there was a bonfire that you could see burning way up on the hill. And a deer was found in the eastern field with twelve stone blades driven into it, a ritual, but it failed to kill the creature, which at least died free."

The woman fixed me with a somber gaze. "You think you know how you'll manage your child. You'll feed her and clothe her, teach her to walk, to read, send her to school. Lena was an early reader. She was sounding out words at four, reading at five. Once, we were playing hide-and-seek, and I could not find her. I was just starting to panic when she appeared at the back door. I was very angry and told her that she was not allowed to go outside alone, and she said, 'But Mummy, I wasn't alone. I was with the Mad Hatter.' Clever little girl. I couldn't be angry at that, even though we were reading *Alice* together and hadn't reached the bit about the Hatter yet, and I knew she'd been looking ahead. I told myself there was no reason to be concerned, but then I saw him."

"Saw who?"

"A man at the far edge of the field. I was hanging out the laundry in the early morning and there was still a blanket of haze on the fields, nothing but birdsong really. But then I saw him. The wheat was waist-high, and he stood completely still in the windswept grain. He was a distance away, so I could not make out his face, but he was wearing a strange tall hat. I wondered how long he'd been watching me. I called to my husband to come, but he didn't hear, so I went in to get him. But by the time we were outside, the man had disappeared. I wanted to call the police, but my husband pointed out that there was no law against standing in a field, that children made things up.

"But I started noticing a change in Lena. She had been such a cheerful girl, but with the appearance of the man, she seemed more withdrawn. When I asked her to describe him, she wouldn't. She was angry with me for not letting her play outside alone anymore, but what could I do? Of course, it was worse after she had to leave school, after the Parson boy died."

"I'm sorry. I don't understand."

"Timothy Parson. He stepped in front of a bus when on an excursion. It was in all the papers."

"I didn't hear about it. I just moved here." I wasn't sure if the woman wanted me to ask questions or expressly did not. An insistent wind was rattling the casements. "What did that have to do with your daughter?"

"Lena was a classmate. The boy was a bully, and she'd complained about him. After he died, the other children wouldn't play with her. The teachers thought she might be traumatized and suggested she finish the year out at home. So it was just the two of us then. She used to beg to go outside, but how could I let her out? Nuneham House was just across the fields. But we went for walks, went to Sandford Lock to feed the ducks. The summer was drawing to a close.

"My husband and I argued over Lena's returning to school. I thought she should stay at home another year. But her father didn't want her slipping further behind. I could see that he was acting in Lena's best interests, but I knew he was wrong. Still, you have to obey your husband." Here she laughed, and it was chilling. "Lena said she hated school. She said the children were mean to her, and she was right. Lena said she hated us both, kicked and screamed, said she'd never go back. We couldn't make her. It took some time to calm her, but she finally settled down. She grew strangely quiet. Her father said he'd take her for a walk, out across the fields, to the village for an ice cream. My husband never came home again."

I waited for her to explain, listening to the steady thrumming of the gutter, exercised by rain.

"I didn't understand until several weeks later. Lena and I were at Sandford Lock, feeding the ducks. There's a plaque up for the two boys who drowned. I saw Lena reading the plaque and as I'd heard the story, I told her what I knew. Of how it had happened long ago, of how the boy had gotten stuck in the current and that the other boy had drowned trying to save him.

"Lena was the most beautiful child, doll-like, with an impish smile that made most everyone laugh. When she smiled, she would sometimes look at me out of the corner of her eye with a sort of knowing that was at odds with someone that age. And she looked that way then and said, 'Mummy, you are telling the story all wrong.'

"I suppose you're wondering what happened to my husband. Well, he and Lena were coming back across the fields and something spooked the cows. They can be quite aggressive in the spring. My husband must have tripped while trying to run away. He was trampled and suffered terribly in the hospital for two days before he finally died. Lena was untouched. When I asked what had happened, she wasn't sure. She said the cows had just run around her. And when I asked her what she'd done, she said she'd done nothing. I wanted to believe her. We want to believe our children. But that day on Sandford Lock, when I was telling Lena about the two poor boys who drowned, she said that I had it all wrong. She said, 'Mummy, what about the third boy?' And I said, 'What third boy?' She replied, 'The one that made them do it.' I said, 'Made them do what?' And she said, 'Made them go in the water, because he didn't like them.'"

I must say that at that point of my visit, had she offered me a cup of tea, I would have refused. "I'm sorry, but I don't understand."

"Isn't that it? Isn't it the truth that we none of us can understand? How can a child achieve such power? And once she has it, how can she be so cruel? She did not want to go back to school. My husband knew to avoid that field at this time of year. Can't you see? Can't you see?" The woman had reached her beautiful hands across the table as if begging me for something. "I didn't want to be responsible, but when you're a mother . . . I wanted to protect Lena but didn't know how."

I struggled for a response, but everything seemed inadequate. I asked, "How old is Lena now?"

"Lena? She's dead, drowned in the lock."

I was getting ready to make my excuses and take my chances with the rain-soaked doorway when the woman got up suddenly and went out of the room. I sat at the little table for what must have been five minutes, then, without making my goodbyes, went back down the hallway. I could hear her upstairs sobbing pathetically and was relieved that she was so emotional as it freed me from a frivolous politeness.

It was still drizzling when I broke through the hedge and began, in my bare feet, to walk back to the barn, when a car pulled up behind me. I was very happy to see Pandora—my neighbor and someone who was to become a close friend—leaning out the window of her Mini. She asked, "Why are you wandering about in your bare feet?"

A short while later, I was sitting in her living room in a pair of her wooly socks in front of the fire, enjoying a cup of strong black tea.

"You look quite worn out," she said.

"I am. It's so sad about that woman."

"Who?"

"Up the lane, about her daughter drowning and her husband being trampled by cows. I didn't even know that happened. So horrible and tragic."

"Yes, it was really. Apparently, it was the talk of the town at the time. She was convicted, you know, for drowning her child. She pushed the little girl in, who I think was only six years old and couldn't swim. She kept calling out for her mother to get her, but the woman didn't move. Sometimes the little girl shows up. Boaters think she's swimming up at them or in the lane—"

"What do you mean she was convicted?"

"The mother? Convicted and hanged. I don't think that would happen now. We'd call it mental illness. One of Bob's colleagues actually wrote a paper on it, something to do with neopagan rituals and group hysteria. She tied it in with the Salem witch trials. My goodness, you've gone all pale. Are you all right?"

Of course I went straight to the house, still in the socks, and yes, it was overgrown. It seemed as if no one had been in there in years. I crept around the back to peer in the window to the kitchen, not knowing if it would be more terrifying to see my host or to discover that she had never been there. The kitchen was empty and looked as if it had not been occupied for some time. The pinch pot, still above the stove, was knitted to the wall with cobwebs.

That evening your father came home. The rain had picked up and he was soaking wet. "You have to call the police," he said. I'd never seen him so frightened. He had been driving home when a little girl appeared right in front of the car. The water was streaming off her and she looked quite blue with cold, her eyes wide with what looked to him—in that instant—like anger. He hit the brakes, but he was convinced he must have struck her. He'd been searching around, calling out, and this had drawn the vicar from his house across the way. He told your father to just go home. To not worry about it. He was sure that no girl had been hit. The rain and light—refraction and all that—played tricks on one's eyes. Your father was surprised at the vicar's lack of surprise. If anything, he seemed oddly resigned in his demeanor. A policeman did come and take a statement, but even he seemed perfunctory in his manner.

Of course, your father went and checked out the house himself, dug up the paper written by the neighbor's colleague, and there really had been some sort of pagan cult set up in the manor house all those years ago. But there's something silly about paganism, about singing at the moon and dressing up in robes and dancing around with antlers on your head, so it was hard to be fearful of it. I did think I saw a man once standing in the yard, but I turned for just a second to see that you were still asleep on the blanket, and when I looked back, the man had vanished and there was nothing to confirm he'd ever been there, just wavering wheat stalks and the hiss of wind across the field, the patter of birdsong, a nodding daffodil, a yellow sun.

Harm

———◆———

I.

Margaret had made the reservation the previous spring, early, when the sabbatical was first approved. She might have canceled but couldn't think of a good reason not to go. No. That wasn't it. She had no energy to do anything and canceling the residency seemed somehow more difficult than attending. She packed her bag for the month and cleared the closet in Lucien's room for the grad student who would be house-sitting. There was a plane to Dublin, a bus to County Monaghan, and then a taxi to the Cabbot House nestled in the hills abutting Newbliss. She packed a raincoat and rain pants so she could walk in all weather and brought the rough draft of *The Circle*, a play about sisters hitting middle age and fighting like children. And now she had a view through the long windows of the second floor across a green lawn inter-rupted by two clean swaths of manicured gravel.

From her window she could see a lake of such glassy stillness that the tall trees on the opposite shore reflected exactly on its surface. A swan floated near the far bank, occasionally upending itself in pursuit of some secret thing.

There was a shifting roster of twelve residents, with departures and arrivals mostly happening on Sunday. The focus was on solitude. There were no presentations of work in progress. Residents gestured vaguely at their projects and the sense was that all shared the same labor and that it was hard and—since they were real artists and writers—they knew better than to provide details about unfinished pieces.

At the dinners—which one had to attend—discussion focused on the weather, Irish feuds in the world of literature, and the different paths that dead-ended into brambles and blackberries and bogs as you tried to circumnavigate the lake. There were silences and, in their tenure, she worried that maybe her tragic tale had crossed the Atlantic. The world of artists and writers was often very small. People talked about the ghost, a Miss Wilbersham, who occupied the room next door to hers and was either jilted at the altar or buried against her wishes. Or perhaps both.

"They say she's friendly," said Kevin, a writer for Irish television. "There's our Margaret, the skeptical American. I suppose you don't believe in ghosts, all of that, things that go bump in the night."

"On the contrary," said Margaret. "I believe in all of it." She wanted to turn the phrase back on him. Of the ten at table, the majority wrote and had quick wits, but nothing came to her.

If the dinners had not been required, Margaret would have skipped them. Her room was tidy and effort had been made to make it cozy, but there was a chill to it, maybe just the result of people shuttling through its walls without ever fully taking residence, though that cold blue aura suited her. She felt beside herself, that when people said someone was "beside herself" it missed the exactness of the phrasing, which was so precise in its sensation. She had to hold it together, at least for Lucien, who needed her. Thankfully, Lucien was settled, miraculously okay, and doing well in his first year at Brown.

II.

Lucien had somehow weathered the horrors of the last six months, although the college application process—so minor in retrospect—had threatened to undo him. It was a tremendous relief when he got in as an early action applicant the previous December, but the application process had been fraught.

Some of it was Max, who had given endless fatherly advice and provided, in detail, his own experiences: SAT scores and interviews and his entering Columbia, which had been his first choice. Max was ostensibly helping Lucien by sharing his knowledge, but Lucien felt under attack. She'd watched Lucien's distress as Max explained how he'd aimed high and hit every mark. That's why she decided to take Lucien to visit colleges to which his father had never applied.

"How about Wexler?" she said. The college counselor was of the opinion that Lucien would get in. "We can stay with Miriam and Ted."

Miriam and Ted lived three hours away, in the town of Langville. The two families were close, but they hadn't all been together in nearly a year. Max had wanted to join the trip to Ted and Miriam's but couldn't. The student art exhibition was going up the next day and Max would be in the gallery hanging paintings all night, provided they were done whitewashing the walls.

"Tell Ted to come here and see me soon," Max said. "He could use a break."

When the kids were small and the couples were in their thirties, they had made a point of getting together every few months: a visit after Thanksgiving, a secular Easter gathering, a few days clustered together in August. Shelly and Lucien played well with each other, even though Shelly was two years older. And then there were the rocky years when Miriam was drinking—although they were all drinking and at the time Margaret had wondered what made Miriam's drinking so special. Ted, in his usual pared-down way, said to her as they shared one of his cigarettes, "Marriage is work, but sometimes it's a lot of work." She wasn't close to Ted and she decided that this is why he'd chosen her to speak to instead of Max, his friend since high school, and someone— didn't she know it—who let no such statement slide without inquiry.

Max had wondered if Ted and Miriam might divorce and spoke about the tragedy of failed marriages. Then there was the surprising news that Miriam was again pregnant, and the drinking was left behind along with the possibility of ending the marriage. When Geraldine was born, she had problems. These were problems that were not to be cured but rather addressed, work by both parents on a schedule that would bind them to the end of their days.

Lucien and Margaret had spent the drive to Langville exchanging movie plots, rewriting endings. Lucien was extremely chatty when his father wasn't around. Over dinner, conversation circled in a pleasant way, Lucien sharing that he wasn't sure where he wanted to go or what he wanted to study. Shelly was now at Tisch in New York. She was a stunning girl with Ted's long limbs and Miriam's cheekbones and cornflower blue eyes. She was studying acting and directors—older men in general. Thus far, it hadn't hurt her and she was doing very well.

Geraldine didn't speak, but Miriam felt compelled to wheel her around and keep her close. Geraldine should really have been in a home, although neither of her parents was willing to admit this. Miriam had her sainthood that she enacted through baths and feedings and her compromised life. Ted seemed to operate out of pity for Miriam. He was still painting his great abstract oils and these were still selling. Miriam had stopped working long ago. First, she'd abandoned the piano to support the household by working admissions at the college. And that she'd abandoned to care for Geraldine. Ted was now tenured and everything would have been easy if it were not so monumentally difficult.

That night, as Margaret recalled, Geraldine had already been put to bed. Lucien excused himself and headed for the basement with his laptop. Miriam made a cup of rooibos tea. "Anyone else?" Miriam said.

Margaret had raised her glass, which was still half-full of wine, and said, "Still working on this."

Ted had a glass of whiskey.

"Have a glass for me," Miriam said. Then Miriam headed up to bed.

"What are you working on?" she asked.

"I can show you. It's big and oily."

Ted's studio was in the barn, a loft that he had renovated himself and managed to heat, although poorly. As Margaret made her way up the steps, which were closer to a ladder, she realized that she was unsteady. It was a red-wine drunk, so her feet went out before her mind. She wasn't about to say anything embarrassing. And even if she did, it was just Ted.

She looked at the painting and said, "That's a lot of red."

Ted looked to the painting, then back to her. He shrugged. "Maybe I'm angry."

She gave Ted a look of rugged sympathy. "Maybe I'm angry too."

On the way back to the house, she felt Ted's hand on her shoulder. He'd turned her to face him and there, behind the house, between the barn and the back porch, he kissed her.

Margaret drove back from Ted and Miriam's in near silence, which Lucien failed to notice as his girlfriend was giving him trouble and he spent most of the trip involved in an epic text messaging exchange. She replayed the kiss in her mind, her adrenaline racing. She wondered if she were falling in love and then decided no. She was headed for disaster, and that surging pulse was an animal instinct alerting her that she was ensnared, in peril. But wasn't it, given circumstance, the same thing?

III.

There was someone new at the coffee machine, and he was baffled by it.

"Can I help?" Margaret asked. The coffee machine at the Cabbot House had various buttons that promised different things. "Do you want an Americano? That's what I usually get."

"I'll take an Americano, if that's what's available." He winked at her. He was Irish, young, and gay.

She said, "There's nothing here but coffee and work."

His name was Conor and he sculpted birds with massive wingspans and heavy legs and feet: things that ought to have been able to fly but couldn't, things that struggled against their own gravity. He was hoping to cast his latest piece in bronze. She asked him how he was going to vent it and if he was concerned about the wingspan given the weight of bronze. "Those are good questions," he said.

"My husband was an artist." Margaret saw Conor's eyes dart down to her ring finger, where she still wore the band. He was thinking, *There's a story here.*

Margaret brought the coffee back up to her room. She looked across the lake to the field that rose sharply from the water's edge and in this field were cows who, at different moments, mooed—contentedly or existentially—stood still, or moved off. Sometimes a calf would race around, although from this distance it could well have been a dog. Older bovines seemed to have abandoned such behavior. She kept hoping that one of her walks would lead her to that enchanted field of cows. This thought did not make her feel particularly special as there were many paintings of cows around the house: other residents had found cows compelling. Even in her room, there were two paintings of two cows, a pairing of pairs. Perhaps these artists had made it across the lake and she might too. Although what view would she have but of the house, and would the distance make it seem more attractive?

That evening, the Cabbot House residents gathered for dinner. Kevin, who seemed to be searching for inspiration, looked around the table. He was drawn to the comic and the depressing, which, apparently, was reflected in his work. "So has anyone seen the ghost?" he asked.

"Why do you ask?" asked Carol. Carol was a famous poet and projected status, although what she'd written was not widely known.

"I heard someone crashing around the room next to mine at about three in the morning." Kevin took a scoop of fish pie and examined its presence on his plate.

"That was me," said Craig. He was Australian, a film-maker. "I'd just come in. Sorry if I woke you up."

"Margaret," said Kevin. "You look like you might have seen something."

She must have been pale. "Nothing supernatural. I find the living quite scary enough."

But she had seen something—or someone, rather. The room that she was staying in, the Butler Room, had the two long windows at the right side of the topmost floor and these she had opened, as she did first thing in the morning. After a quick coffee, she'd gone for a stroll along the lake, joined by the small black dog whose house she passed on the way. Margaret was walking back up the lawn when she happened to glance up at the windows. At this time of day, the sun slanted sharply onto the desk. And that's when she saw him—or thought she did. A person standing in her room, but who was it? She could see the outline of a figure in a bulky coat, the head tilted to one side, but it was a shadowy figure with few details. She felt convinced that it was Max.

IV.

Several months after Lucien's college visit, Margaret had returned to Langville. It was a Tuesday night and she was to speak at Wexler the next day. Annika, a former student, was teaching a class there and had assigned her play *Happy Victims*. She was to stay with Ted and Miriam. Max had to teach the next day, so he was unable to join her. She did not see Miriam's car. Ted opened the door in the green shaker knit sweater, his favorite. The elbows were bulging on it and the hem was fraying. "Your sweater seems to be returning to its origins," she said.

"Ah, like an unstable compound. In another five years it will be a sheep." He stepped back from the door and ushered her in. She wanted to hug him but didn't. Instead she took his hand, as if to read his palm, then curled his fingers into a fist. He seemed pleased by the gesture but did not reciprocate.

"Where's Miriam?" she asked.

"Hospital. They think Geraldine might have aspirated some water into her lungs."

Margaret nodded as if she knew what it meant. Ted did not seem worried. She followed him into the kitchen and he opened the refrigerator. "Are you hungry?" he asked. "There's some salmon in here. Or I could make you an egg."

"Are you a good cook, Ted?"

"No. But even bad cooks can make decent eggs."

"Wine, please," she said.

She sipped her wine while Ted recounted a story from childhood, about a trip that he and his brother had taken to Scotland during college. They had backpacked around and Ted had decided there to pursue painting. His telling had a nervous rattle. "Why in Scotland?" she asked.

"I have no idea. I just did. And here I am." He gestured around the kitchen.

When she was done with her glass of wine, Ted excused himself to his studio. She watched him leave, following him to the sink and then into the hallway with her eyes. When she was brushing her teeth, she heard him by the stairs on the phone with Miriam. He said, "Don't worry. Margaret's already gone to bed. If you think the nurse is subpar, you should stay at the hospital." She heard him toss his phone onto a surface and then take the first step to the upstairs. But then he stopped. There was a sigh and then the creaking of floorboards along the corridor. She could hear him paused in front of the guest bedroom as she quietly rinsed her mouth. Something had shifted between them and her nerves were electrified. She didn't move and soon his footsteps retreated back up the hall.

As she drove home heading east along the turnpike, Margaret thought about Max. What had drawn them together? Most of her girlfriends were attracted to him, liked the dirty blond mane and Viking features. He looked like fun and was and this charmed them. He wore Converse and jeans and blazers. In the early nineties, that was good. He dressed the same way now, out of deference—perhaps— to his younger self. She and Max had a class together, even though his degree was in fine arts and hers an MFA with a concentration in poetry. The class was on early film. He would sit behind her in the dark room, and she could feel his eyes on the back of her head. His confidence was alarming. Girls liked Max because he was attractive and made them feel pretty. Guys liked Margaret because she was strange and made them feel interesting. She still wasn't sure why she and Max had married so young. Maybe their faculties were clouded by all the alcohol they consumed. But she also knew from this skewed vantage point, in love (because what else was it?) with Ted, that she was most likely rewriting the past.

V.

Margaret was walking away from the lake, as that was the route the dog had chosen. The path was graveled in two neat tracks and cut through woodlands and glades carpeted with moss. Perfect daisies were stitched on the grassy borders. The dog had slipped from sight. There was a chill to the day and Margaret had no gloves with her. The gloves were still in the suitcase as the previous days had been warm. She was pulling the sleeves of her sweater over her knuckles when she felt herself observed. There at the end of the path, she saw the figure. It had to be Max, because she recognized the barn jacket as his. She had just processed the impossibility of what she was seeing when the figure stepped from the path and, even though this movement would not have concealed it, on stepping vanished from view. Perhaps her eyes were playing tricks on her. She had certainly had enough wine the night before and that, along with a good number of Kevin's cigarettes, had made her feel raw and nervous in the morning. But she knew the jacket, even though the face of the figure had been obscured as if in deep shadow. Margaret had worn that coat to get the paper on Sunday mornings as it was always on a peg in the mudroom when it wasn't on Max. Max often worked in that coat and her hands would emerge from the pockets smudged with charcoal. The pockets harbored bits of rag, shreds of tobacco, and a powdery residue that combined all the former with lint. The coat was still hanging on its peg in the mudroom. After his death, she had wrapped herself in it, refusing to take the jacket off until Lucien asked her to. And she did, because she could not explain that she still loved Max, and hated him, and that this intensity of feeling that might also be shame was pulsing with extreme vibrancy, as if she had taken Max's life and folded it into hers—as if she were a splitting atom. She had looked at the jacket before she left the house, taking a moment as the airport shuttle turned in her driveway. *That's what's left of Max*, she had thought.

At least the Miss Wilbersham room was finally occupied. Margaret hoped that another body in the next room would dispel some of the charged emptiness that she felt while moving through her study and bedroom. She hoped her neighbor would be restless because the utter stillness of the night made it difficult to sleep. The woman had shown up with a thousand pages of unedited manuscript that she hoped to blow through in the next three weeks. Her name was Maeve, and she was polite but clearly hassled. Even her handshake seemed rushed—a clamp of cold fingers quickly withdrawn. Margaret tried to think of a way to tell Maeve that her room was haunted but knew that she would come off as desperately genial or odd, so she said nothing. Margaret, too, would be too busy for idle chitchat.

The following morning she ran into Maeve by the refrigerator. Maeve fixed her with an odd look, as if tempted to say something but then thinking better of it.

"How was your first night?" she asked.

Maeve replied, "I was awoken at around four o'clock and couldn't get back to sleep." Maeve's look seemed accusing and she wondered if Maeve might be a very light sleeper. She made a note not to flush the toilet when she got up during the night.

VI.

Max and Margaret were driving to Ted and Miriam's house on a Friday evening. Lucien was staying by himself, which meant with his girlfriend, who would have told her parents she was staying with a friend. Margaret didn't care as long as there wasn't a party. Margaret's overnight case was on the back seat of the car. Max had wanted to share a bag since they were only going for the one night and found her insistence on having her own somehow provoking. Why didn't she want to share? She wanted to respond, *Because I'm in love with Ted.* She said instead, "I don't need a reason to want my own bag." As they drove west, Max kept glancing at her. She looked at the woods and signs and tried to think of something to say. She imagined the car skidding off the road and into a ravine. Would that kill her? She imagined stepping from the wreck in bare feet because to imagine herself dead was just to see herself sleeping, her head on the wheel, although she wasn't driving. She wondered what had happened, in the fantasy, to her shoes.

"So how's *The Circle?*" asked Max.

"Fucking pain in the ass." She managed a gruesome smile. "I hate the characters and they hate me."

Ted was really Max's friend, someone he'd known since high school. They were more like brothers than friends. Max could have been anything—a doctor, a lawyer, a politician.

Max had decided to be an artist, but Ted could only paint. In college, Max had gained quite a reputation for his talent because he was smart and dynamic and fun and worked hard. His work was good, but Margaret had always resisted it. At first she'd thought this was because Max might crush her with his intensity if she couldn't create distance, but later she realized that it was because she found Max's work soulless. She could always see the influence of someone—a little Blake in the figures and composition, a little Dalí in the barren landscape, some Turner in the swirling light. She wondered if Max would ever create a piece that was not referential. She had only survived beside him because of her utter faith in her own work—her sense that her work was worth something before anyone else had seen it, which Max would never fully understand.

Or was she thinking this now because of Ted? Had she thought this before?

She had met Ted shortly after she and Max started dating. Max organized a party with the usual grad school crowd and Ted spent the weekend sleeping with Blaire Holcomb, who was also in poetry and unattached at the time. Max was dismissive of Ted with an edgy focus that immediately communicated to Margaret how much he admired Ted's work. She understood that Max wanted Ted to like her. Ted's attentive demeanor let her know that she was unlike Max's other girlfriends. Being with Ted, she realized that Max was in love with her.

After graduate school, she had published her first and last book of poems. On a whim, she wrote a play and sent it, also on a whim, to a fellowship program. She was surprised when she received the award and also when the play was produced to some acclaim. The job market was dire, and when she and Max both managed to get positions at a small arts college in the Berkshires, it seemed like a sign. They married and were still teaching at that same institution.

And Ted had moved to Red Hook, where he met Miriam, who was a roommate in the house he shared with five other people.

Max had worked connections to get Ted his first teaching job, but now it was Ted who had the better connections. For a moment she felt sorry for Max, but something signaled to her that she would not be sorry for him always. Something had been handed back to her. The subversion of her love for Ted had created little fissures. She felt possessed, then realized she really was, possessed by that self that had existed before Max. Why was she, suddenly, so angry?

Miriam greeted them at the door. Geraldine had just been fed and Ted was getting her ready for bed. The house smelled of spice and effort, a complicated Szechuan lamb that Miriam had cooked up because she was a good cook and Margaret wasn't. Margaret sipped her wine listening to Miriam expound on the joys of mint tea. Max was flirting with Miriam in a generous way and Miriam was basking in it. When Ted appeared at the threshold of the kitchen, Margaret had a sudden urge to tears, and he caught her eye and understood. She and Ted were quiet through the meal, watching as Max tended to Miriam with gentle flattery and alluded to Miriam's dark, sexy side, which didn't exist. Max started talking about a long-ago camping trip and somehow conversation led to the time he and Margaret had sex on a train. Margaret said, "Are you sure that was me?" Which was funny but truthful, because although she had the memory, she didn't really believe that she'd ever done that. She also wondered why Max was so inclined to talk about incidents in their sex life. Was he sensing something?

Max, of course, volunteered to help Miriam clean up. Margaret went out to bum one of Ted's cigarettes, which were in the studio. She went up the ladder first, feeling Ted's eyes on her back. In the studio, he wrapped his arms around her. He was nearly a foot taller and had to bend to do this. She rested her cheek on his chest, listening hard, as if something other than a heartbeat might lurk within.

Ted asked, "Are you good at this sort of thing?"

She asked, "What sort of thing is this?"

He furrowed his brows. His narrow nose divided his face knifelike, the right eye slightly higher than the left. Her blood was up. "It's nothing yet," he said.

She tugged on the hem of his sweater and watched her hands take his sweater over his bowed head. "And now?" she demanded.

Ted watched her with his dark icon eyes. He tugged his T-shirt down, covering the ridge of black hair that had, for a moment, been exposed. "I'm just so tired," he said.

She nodded because that made sense. She started to unbuckle his belt.

"I can't take them anymore," she said. Even she wasn't even sure who *they* were. "I want to blow everything up." She slipped his belt through the loops with one quick tug and threw it on the floor, the buckle clanging hard on the broad boards.

VII.

Near the end of Maeve's first week of the residency, Margaret was surprised to see her moving her things out of the Miss Wilbersham room. Maeve was taking another down the corridor and near the back stairs, although it did not have a view of the lake, which she had, at first, wanted.

"My room was just a bit noisy," said Maeve, but she was clearly being guarded.

"I don't hear anything at all in my room," said Margaret. "It's silent as the tomb."

"To each his own," Maeve replied. This statement was in response to nothing or an incorrect response to something. Regardless, it was irrelevant to their exchange. She wondered why Maeve didn't like her. The two had hardly interacted.

Later, when she was printing out a few pages in the computer room, she heard Maeve chuckling with someone, someone Maeve did like. Maeve said, "It was the oddest thing. There was someone standing at the end of my bed, and I could've sworn it was that American writer, Margaret. Next day I checked the door and I'd locked it. But I swear she was standing at the end of my bed."

Margaret stood as the last of her pages printed and heard the door to the back stairs slam as Maeve and the unseen friend returned to their rooms. Although she had clearly done nothing, she still felt somehow embarrassed by what Maeve had said.

VIII.

Margaret was visiting her mother in Hoboken. Her father had been moved to the nursing home back in April, after he fell and broke his hip.

She drove from her mother's house to a parking garage on Seventy-Sixth and Amsterdam, near the hotel where she was meeting Ted. He was standing by the bar when she came in. Her joy at seeing his lanky, stooped figure surprised her.

She registered the silver streaks in his black hair and that his shirt was overlarge. He'd become gaunt over the last few years—she'd noticed as it happened—and with his sharp cheekbones and pooling eyes, he looked like a mystic, someone who might cry out in a long-ago desert. She realized that nothing was casual with Ted. Also, that she hadn't shrugged off her passivity but merely traded one role for an another. Ted likely thought her in charge. They were both damning each other in this way.

They took a bottle of wine to the room. The bed made both of them nervous. She took off all her clothes and stood on one side, naked and challenging. He took off all his clothes and stood opposite her, the bed between them.

Ted was showering when the phone began to buzz. She looked over out of habit. It was Miriam. The phone quieted but then shortly after buzzed again. She wondered if Miriam was that sort of person who hated it when people didn't pick up her calls. The phone buzzed again. And there was another buzzing. Her phone. Ted came out of the bathroom wearing a towel. They stood in silence, listening to the phones buzzing.

Margaret drove home with a quiet mind. Methodically, she went through the matter of her life. Max had grown around her like a vine. She felt choked by him, but he depended on her. His love was a real and terrible thing. Snow started to fall as if to confirm this. When she reached the house, she could see Max sitting at the table through the kitchen window. He was still sitting at the table when she entered the house, even though he must have heard her car in the drive. She stood in the hallway, at the threshold of the kitchen.

Max said, "How long has this been going on?"

She said, "How long has what been going on?"

Max said, "Don't lie to me, Margaret."

She said, "You had the affair with the student."

Max said, "You didn't care." He said this with genuine anguish.

She tried to think of some dishonest thing to say that might make everything better but drew a blank.

Max said, "How could you do this to Lucien?"

She hadn't felt she was doing anything to Lucien, but maybe she was. She did not feel guilt, only a sort of relief.

"Say something," said Max. A moment passed. "But of course you won't because you don't feel that you need to." Max stood from the table. He took his keys from the counter. She heard the front door slam shut and the sound of Max's car in the driveway. She felt incapable of movement. She knew Max must be driving to Ted and Miriam's house. It was very like Max to think this was to be resolved with Ted, that this was between the two men. There was a glass and a bottle of Maker's Mark on the table, half-empty. The bottle had been in the cabinet for months. She couldn't remember how full it had been.

IX.

At dinner, Margaret was seated beside an American woman, a textile artist, whom she had been avoiding since she arrived the day before. The woman's name was Hannah and something about her seemed familiar. She offered Hannah a glass of wine out of politeness. Hannah fixed her with a look. "You don't remember me. It's been years." She didn't remember Hannah and found it strange that Hannah did not immediately supply the details. After the dessert plates were cleared, Hannah took another glass of wine and topped up Margaret's glass. The other artists and writers were going for a walk by the lake, but the full glass of wine made it awkward for her to join them. When they were gone, Hannah said, "I roomed with Ted and Miriam in the house in Red Hook."

Margaret remembered. She had met Hannah a long time ago and then again more recently—in the last ten years.

"I heard about Max. I am so sorry."

She did not know how to respond. She looked at her wedding band.

"Look, I know you've been in the shit, but I have to say I know Miriam, and I knew her and Ted back then. He was my friend. Ted was going to break up with Miriam, and then all of a sudden she was pregnant." Hannah reached around to help herself to one of the other writers' bottles. "Everyone's always going on about how Miriam's such a saint and how could Ted do that to her, but it's bullshit. He never wanted to marry her in the first place."

Margaret didn't know what to say. She nodded and nodded again. She took Hannah's hand and held it.

"And," Hannah continued, "Miriam kept drinking when she was pregnant with Geraldine. I was in town to see Ted's show and I saw her in a parked car by the BiLo drinking from the bottle. I don't know why she bothered to hide. Ted knew but couldn't figure out what to do about it."

Margaret walked to the lake. It was a clear night and the lights from the house were enough to guide her. She couldn't find the moon, but the stars were many and brilliant. Ted had called her the day of Max's funeral. Of course, he couldn't attend. She thought the only people there should have been Miriam, Ted, and her. Even Lucien seemed somehow irrelevant to the proceedings. She'd answered the phone with silence. Ted said, "I feel I've abandoned you."

Margaret said, "You don't have a choice."

She'd actually felt a physical pain in her chest to hear his voice, to know he could not save her. To know whatever they had shared would not grow, would be nothing but a sordid note or point of glee in the stinking stir of gossip. She said, "What if I love you?"

Ted said, "What if we love each other?"

In the background she could hear Geraldine's guttural shouting.

Margaret stared across the lake to the opposite shore where the pasture sharply sloped upward from the water's edge. This was the pasture with the picturesque cows, the pasture she had been trying to reach through various trails throughout the week. Her efforts had led into swampy places and brambles, to a lone bull who marked her progress around the fence with unsettling attention. There was a sound of rattling and she realized it had started to rain. The rattling was the percussive music of drops hitting the surface of the lake. She took her shoes off first and then her socks. She was in jeans that were too big since she'd lost ten pounds in the last month. The jeans slid down her legs along with her underwear. She pulled her sweater over her head with the T-shirt still in it. She unhooked her bra and threw it onto the pile. The sky was bright with stars and even though she could not see the moon from where she stood, she felt sure that somewhere it was full or close to full and lighting her way. The water was cold on her feet. She felt alert, as if she had woken from a bad dream. She wanted to see the house from the opposite side of the lake, to be with the cows, to look at something from a distance and have it make sense.

X.

Jennifer was in her first morning at the Cabbot House. She was staying in the Butler Room, which was next to the Miss Wilbersham room. The view to the lake was astoundingly beautiful, and she had been happy watching the cows for close to an hour before she felt the need to get some coffee. She wondered if she would get any work done. Conor, a sculptor, was by the coffee maker, and she waited for him to be done with his coffee selection. At first he didn't notice her, but she watched him. She found him attractive, although she thought he was gay. He was working on a large piece in one of the studios, a raven with an enormous wingspan that he would cast in bronze.

"Didn't see you there," he said, his cup in hand.

"I'm not sure if I'm supposed to say anything to people before dinner."

"You can talk to me," he said. He took a seat at the table. There was a basket and he unfolded a napkin in it revealing freshly baked scones. "They're still warm."

"I might join you for just a minute, if it's all right." Jennifer hit the button for a coffee and the machine responded with impressive grinding followed by a slow, productive trickle.

"How's your room?" he asked.

"Beautiful, with a great view." She sat with her coffee and put a scone on a plate. "I hear it's haunted, but no one's bothered me."

"It is haunted," said Conor, "by a woman who appears in a brown jacket."

"Is there a good story?"

Conor nodded. His eyes were twinkling. "It's the ghost of an American playwright. She drowned in the lake. She'd had a bit to drink. Apparently she decided to go for a swim, although it was the middle of the night and very cold. Her clothes were right out front, by the bench. She'd made friends with a dog, that little black one you see hanging around, and it led its owner to the body."

"That's horrifying."

"Yeah. I actually met her here, two years ago. Her name was Margaret."

"What was she like?"

"She seemed nice enough but was kind of subdued. It was right after her husband died. Apparently, she'd been having an affair with his best friend, a painter, and the husband, also a painter, found out about it and drove off in a snowstorm after consuming the better part of a bottle of whiskey. He hit a tree and was dead instantly."

Jennifer was thoughtful. She said, "Were they in love?"

"Who?"

"The friend and this Margaret. Where they in love?"

"Maybe they were," said Conor. "But in the end, it doesn't really matter, does it? In another twenty years, we'll all have forgotten who she was. She'll just be that lady buried in the wrong place, another ghost wandering about, desperate for someone to supply the narrative."

"I say it had to be love," said Jennifer. "Why else would she do that?"

Conor nodded appreciatively and it was moving, this impossible love of a dead woman, a dead love, a tale of few concrete details except for its irrepressible woe.

The Flowers,
the Birds, the Trees

On the wall opposite was the picture of Saint Michael, his foot pressing into the side of Lucifer's head, a spear raised for speedy victory. Jane had often looked at this picture while sitting on the hard seat, contemplating the fate of the wicked. Jane could hear her father's booming, cheery voice quite clearly through the door. And also the measured response.

"It is quite impossible that Jane stay on at Loreto. She is clearly an intelligent girl and a good athlete. But recent events have made her isolated. And frankly, I think she's a danger to the other children."

That was Sister Barry, who had never liked her. Had found her reluctance to smile and join in and let the more cheerful girls win at sports problematic.

"She is just a child," said her father. "One would hate to think that this traffic in rumors has somehow had an effect on your judgment, Sister Barry. Jane has lost her closest friend and I don't think moving her to another school is in her best interests."

"The other children won't play with her. She spends recess and lunchtime alone. She is morose."

"She is grieving and probably traumatized. She saw Clara's death, was sitting right beside her in the tree when she fell. If nothing else, Jane deserves some sympathy here.

One would think that Christian sentiment would lead to an embracing of my daughter. The girl's been through a lot."

"I have to think about what's best for the school."

"All right." Her father's voice had dropped an octave. Niceties had been dispensed with. "Then let's do that."

What followed was a brief discussion about the cost of repairing the roof. Jane's father was on the board of Loreto Nedlands. He was usually too busy to attend the meetings, but he knew his way around expenses. If a problem could be handled with money, Jane's father was the man. The nuns were poor and although that was the way of things for nuns, they did need money. The New Roof Cake Sale had raised fifteen dollars and seventeen cents, not much even by the standards of an eleven-year-old. Jane had stood by the long table laden with misshapen lamingtons and collapsing sponges and would have shared her observation that having one child buy the cake of another child only to have that child return the favor could not possibly create a surplus of money, but no one was there to listen. Her own glorious matchsticks, powdered to perfection having been purchased at a bakery, had gone untouched, as if poisoned. Clara would have bought one, but Clara was dead.

When the office door swung open, Jane knew that her father had won. Sister Barry, too, seemed to hold an aura of victory, but Jane felt the sandal of oppression pressed firmly against her cheek.

"Why don't you have a party?" asked her father on the drive home. "We could hire a clown, get ponies for rides. You could make some new friends."

"That might be nice," she said. How to tell her father that no one would come? He would soon, thank God, forget the idea, have it displaced by some other thing. And she would show up with a ribbon or a trophy for winning something—the hundred meters or backstroke or whatever one could win without being part of a team—and he'd give her that approving nod. And maybe buy her something, a new tennis racket or a bicycle. Or maybe he wouldn't forget and his secretary, Miss Banks, would set the thing up. And the children would come, forced by their parents, who did not want to cross Arthur French, a leading attorney, a powerful man. Jane could see herself in a stiff little dress watching as clowns juggled and children rode ponies and cakes melted in the heat.

Mrs. Glave was sweeping the verandah when they pulled up to the house. As Jane stepped from the car, she could see Mrs. Glave tie and retie her apron, a nervous tic, as the woman's concerned expression bloomed into a loving, straining smile. "So she's back from the trenches," said Mrs. Glave. "And how was it?"

"Fine, thank you," said Jane. She stood by Mrs. Glave, looking down at the tops of her shoes.

"Looks like those could use a polish." Mrs. Glave hooked her hand under Jane's chin, tilting it upward. "I have everything we need to make toffee. How does that sound?"

"No, thank you, Mrs. Glave. I'm not very hungry."

"Well, how about a walk then, down to the shops? You might be hungry after that."

It was clear that Mrs. Glave was not going to give up. "I wouldn't mind going to the shops."

"I can drop you, if you like," said Jane's father. He set his briefcase down on the step, ready with good cheer.

The sympathy of the adults weighed on her shoulders like a shroud.

"I'd rather walk," said Jane.

Mrs. Glave liked a slow walk. And the weather was glorious, wattle in full bloom, a tonic breeze coming off the river. Jane put one foot in front of the other, avoiding the cracks, the old rhyme buzzing darkly through her head: *Step on a crack, break you mother's back.*

"So," said Mrs. Glave, "are you still sad about your friend?"

Jane nodded.

"Well, that was a tragedy. And you don't want too many of those in life. It is a sad thing that one as young as you has suffered through the loss of her mother and her dear friend, and with no brothers or sisters to cheer her up."

"Maybe I don't want to be cheered up," said Jane.

"Right," said Mrs. Glave. "I do remember that feeling. When I was your age, my best friend in the world died, too, only she was my sister. She was eighteen and a lovely, lovely thing. We were so sad in my house, my father, mother, and brothers, all of us weeping. But I had no tears, because my heart had broken, and broken hearts do not let you cry. My heart wouldn't mend. Life went on but not for me. My mother told me to try to cheer up. 'Look at the flowers and the birds and the trees,' she said. 'You know what God's taken away but see what he left behind.'"

"And did you cheer up?"

"Not for a long time. No, Jane. Oh, I was sad and I hated everyone and everything. The food had lost its flavor."

"But you're happy now. Even when you're cleaning the toilets, I can hear you singing."

"But I wasn't for a very long time."

"My father says I'll forget about Clara when I make a new friend."

"Well, for a man who's most often right, I'll have to tell you, he's wrong there. You'll never forget Clara."

"So what will make me happy?"

Mrs. Glave turned away, her face angled to the sky, but Jane—from knowing her—knew this meant she was barreling deep into her past, was probably back in Limerick. She returned to the present and presented Jane with a serious look.

"How did you stop being so sad about your sister?"

"Oh, it was a strange thing, and I'm sure your father wouldn't want me telling you."

But invoking her father's disapproval meant that the battle had already been won. "Well, she came back to me, my Leila did. I woke in the night to find her sitting on the end of my bed. She had her back turned and was brushing her hair. She had beautiful thick hair and would go at it, a hundred strokes every night before bed. I watched her for a while, barely daring to breathe, and then she turned and looked to me."

Jane held her breath.

"She was as beautiful as the day she died, but her eyes had gone quiet, cold. I closed my eyes. I was so frightened. When I opened them again, she was gone. But you could see where she'd been sitting, where the feather bed had been pushed down. And then I willed myself to stop missing her, to stop grieving."

"But why?"

"She came back because I missed her so, and the thought that she might visit again was so terrifying that I decided not to miss her at all!" Mrs. Glave laughed and shook her head. "The dead belong in their place, and the living in ours, and it's best to make peace with that."

But people didn't. Her father hadn't ever gotten over her mother, even though Miss Banks sometimes spent the night, sneaking out before Jane was supposed to be awake.

"Are you worrying about Clara? Because you shouldn't. She's in a place where nothing can hurt her anymore."

"With God, I suppose. That's what you mean, isn't it?"

"Yes, Jane. That is what I mean."

"Well, maybe she is and maybe she isn't. And I don't care either way. And I'm not sad for her. I'm angry."

"Why would you be angry?" asked Mrs. Glave.

"Clara told me she would be my best friend forever. She promised. We made a pact. We—" Jane held back.

"What did you do, Jane?"

"We were friends, that's all, and she left me."

How had Jane forgotten about the hair? It had been Clara's idea, to take two locks and braid them together. There had never been a friendship such as theirs, never. And this gesture, Clara thought, would make the friendship unbreakable. Solemnly, they had knelt by the altar in the chapel. Clara had first snipped off a reasonably small hank of Jane's hair, then Jane had done the same to her. The ends were tied with a blue ribbon, plaited in together, and tied off. The shiny black hair braided in with the coarser red had made a convincing talisman. And there was an oath uttered, something with "forever" and "bond" and "the spirits," and they had shivered together, awed by their purpose, awed by their connection. The girls had placed the plait—that gently curving twist of black and red small enough to fit in the palm of one's hand—beneath the carpet by the altar, which seemed to have an all-purpose sort of sacredness. How long until the plait was found?

In all the madness following Clara's death, Jane had first been in shock and then all she had wanted to do was sleep. She had spent entire days in bed and eaten nothing but soup. Then she had returned to school and the looks of the children, their refusal to partner or play with her, and the adults' complicity in all of this had exhausted any normal thoughts. If they found it, they would ask her about it, no doubt, as her hair was the blackest in the school and Clara's an almost singular red. All those hours she had spent being questioned by the nuns. Why had they been up in the tree? Children were not allowed to climb, and Clara, although being a spirited girl, was most often obedient. Unlike Jane. If they found the hair, they would no doubt see it as some devil thing. They would bring her in again, and the questions would start all over. She was going to have to get it back the next day.

When Jane went to bed, there had been a strong wind. The long-fingered leaves of the ghost gum outside her window had been brushing against the pane, keeping her up, and she'd wondered how she was going to fall asleep. But suddenly, here she was awake, and the house was still. The hallway light pushed around the outline of her bedroom door, which was left a crack open. Before Clara's death, Jane had liked a completely dark room, but she had become nervous as of late, and the slight spill of light that forced its way into the quiet blackness of the room seemed to offer security. She wondered if she had to use the toilet, if that's why she was up, but then she heard someone in the hall—or was it? Maybe it was just that midnight sound that sometimes came from her father's room, as the bedhead knocked against the wall. She listened carefully. Maybe Miss Banks was staying over. Maybe she would giggle, as she sometimes did, and then her father—in a low, kindly grumble—would suffocate that woman voice, that thing he needed that was not Jane, nor her mother. The knocking continued, indeed it seemed to be drawing closer. It was footsteps, although awkward and uneven, as if one leg were being dragged. Jane waited, feeling herself grow cold. The room grew cold, too, as the quiet—that pooling stillness between the footfalls and her own nervous inhalations—was violated by the approaching of each step and a barely audible but persistent, rasping breath. Closer and nearer came the breathing and steps, as if someone were walking slowly up the hall. At the threshold of her door, whatever it was stopped. And then there was stillness. Jane waited, holding her breath for what seemed to be a long time. All was quiet. She allowed herself to exhale. The door, still open a crack and revealing the line of light, then succumbed to a gentle pressure and slid shut with a soft, articulate click.

Jane darted out her hand and switched on her reading lamp. The room was empty, plain, her stuffed rabbit propped in the chair, her books in disorder on the desk, her uniform—tunic, tie, skirt, pinafore—arranged for the following morning on the clothes horse. But she was sure she had heard someone walking to her, limping up the hall, waiting, and then closing the door. It had been Clara.

At recess, the other children were all on the playing fields. Jane, being morose, raised no suspicion by being alone. She hung around the front verandah by the entrance to the chapel, but there was no one around. She tried the knob and found the door unlocked. The chapel was a plain affair, too small for school functions, which were all conducted at Holy Rosary several blocks away. The nuns heard daily Mass in the chapel and, occasionally, classes were gathered here for things like choir practice or catechism. The nuns had their own seats at the front, their own little prayer books, their own little kneeling cushions. The room was bright with midmorning light, cool with a defining gloom. The faces of all the actors in the stations—Simon helping with the cross, Veronica lifting her veil—were all caught in this celebration of misery, marching on to the inevitable and eternally joyless crucifixion. Jesus was suspended right over where Jane needed to be. She looked around to confirm her solitude, but in the corner . . . No! And no. She had panicked catching sight of a figure, but it was just a statue of Mary, serene in her robes, her hands extended at her sides in invitation, but to what? Mrs. Glave had told Jane that Mary was her mother, that any time she wished to speak to her mother, she just had to pray the rosary, but who could believe that? The tabernacle light glowed red.

The plait had been placed beneath the green rug on which the altar rested. Jane knelt quickly and lifted up the corner. She didn't see it and was flooded with panic, but she slid her hand and felt for it, now hearing footsteps coming up the verandah. And then her fingers touched the fine braid and it was in her hand, and—scuttling up—she had just enough time to put it in the pocket of her pinafore and slide into the first pew, to assume the proper look of prayerful attitude, when Sister Enda entered the chapel.

Sister Enda walked up the aisle with a measured step. "Are you praying?" she asked. Jane nodded. In her pocket, she felt the twist of hair, two different textures—slippery and coarse—woven together. Sister Enda stepped into the pew, and Jane slid over on the kneeler to make room for her, but Sister Enda sat down. "I'm avoiding the heat. This is always the coolest spot in the entire school." Sister Enda pulled up her long skirts to her knees and relaxed. "Don't pray too much, Jane. God actually wants us out and about, enjoying things."

Jane moved from the kneeler to the seat. "Sister Enda, can I ask you something?"

"Anything, except why I became a nun. That, my dear, is between me and God." There was a moment of quiet. "Was there something, then?"

Jane edged off the kneeler and sat on the pew. "Do you believe in ghosts?"

Sister Enda moved her gaze from Jane to the altar, considering. "Well, there's the Holy Ghost. But I know that's not what you're asking me, and, frankly, the Holy Ghost is a bit hard to understand." Sister Enda looked around, but the two were quite alone. She pulled off her veil, revealing a line of sweat where the band had touched her forehead. She had very short hair, not like a boy but rough and uneven, as if she'd cut it herself. "Do you remember Sister Iona?"

"She's the one who kept all the budgies." Sister Iona had had a little shed set up by the storeroom where she kept a wall of cages filled with the birds. When Jane was in the early grades, she remembered going to the shed and Sister Iona letting her fill the seed cups. Once, Sister Iona had shut the shed door and let several of the birds out, and they had flown around, landing on the nun's head and on her hands, until she had gently captured them and placed them back in their cages. "They said God had a special purpose for her."

"Sister Iona was mentally retarded, and one of the best God ever made. She died, quite suddenly. There had, apparently, been something amiss with her heart. Well, I don't know if you remember it, but Sister Iona used to ring the bell for the Angelus. And the day she died, in all the hubbub and grief around her death, we didn't remember to assign someone else to do it. But the bell rang all the same."

"Was it Sister Iona?"

"I'm sure of it."

"How can you know?"

"Because I saw her, later that day. She was walking up the long hallway and she smiled at me in her simple way. I didn't immediately understand. I'd forgotten she was dead, but after she passed, I remembered. I turned quickly."

"Had she vanished?"

"No. She was still there, walking up the hall, but her feet . . . She was floating, two inches off the ground."

The hairs were all up on Jane's arms, despite the heat. Sister Enda extended her arm, alive with goose bumps, in solidarity. "But why had Sister Iona come back?"

"I don't know if the dead need a reason. In the case of Sister Iona, she didn't like changing her routine. And she took time to adjust to a new thing, so it might have taken a while for the fact she was dead to actually sink in."

Sister Iona may not have had a good reason to come back, but Clara did. She was good at her schoolwork, particularly English, and did her homework every night. She was one of the girls who always raised her hand in class. The nuns loved her. They thought she could do no wrong. Even when she'd torn her blouse while crawling around in the space under the stage in the Hall—definitely not allowed—the nuns had believed her story, something about the hedges around the grotto, something that involved improbable prayer. Sweet-tempered Clara was actually not sweet-tempered but more fair. She didn't get angry without good reason. She was good-tempered because that was the right way to be, but if something disturbed her sense of justice, Clara reacted. That's how they became friends, back in grade three. The children had been making tissue-paper flowers for Mother's Day. Jane made a lovely pale blue flower, probably the best in the class, and this had drawn the attention of Penny Tilson.

"Are you going to dig a hole in the ground and put it there for your mum? I'm sure she'll love it. She'll put it right beside her pet worm."

Jane had had an impossibility of feeling. Objectively, she thought what Penny had said was funny. But the freakish sadness of it all—her mother's beautiful face beneath the dirt, now probably just a skull—was back again. Her dead mother was something that Jane could forget but never for long. The usually quiet Clara, who had been sitting beside Jane, said, "You are a horrible person, Penny. God isn't going to forget this, and Lucifer is going to get you with his poker. You will burn for a hundred years and not have anything to drink. That's what happens to mean people." A stunning indictment made all the more cutting because it was true.

From that moment, Jane had been loyal to Clara, although Clara had taken a while to win over. Jane was fun in a dangerous sort of way and had courted Clara with invitations to the nuns' quarters, the storeroom, the area by the incinerator where they'd discovered Mr. Duggan's magazines—naked ladies winking over pink shoulders—hidden beneath a milk crate. Eventually, Clara had given up on the other girls. It was always more fun with Jane. But Clara was still liked by everyone and Jane only by those impressed by her athletic prowess and the fancy cakes and chocolates in her lunch. In the summer, Clara came with Jane to York and spent two weeks at the family farm, riding the horse and swimming in the river. On Clara's birthday, Jane had given her a pair of roller skates to match hers, fancy adjustable ones with red leather straps and ball-bearing wheels that hummed when you went at good speed. Clara's parents were unenthusiastic about the gift. Her mother had said, "Oh, well that's very nice, but we really can't accept anything so fancy." Clara, not listening, had put them right on. And of course Clara's parents had felt shown up. They'd given her a book of Bible stories—an expensive one with a stamped leather cover—but who wanted that? Clara and Jane became inseparable. When Clara came down with scarlet fever, Jane had conducted herself in a horror of silence, terrified that Clara would not survive. All the students remembered her in their prayers, but Jane had prayed hardest of all and Clara had recovered. When Clara returned to school, the girls made the pact, sealed with their entwined hair. All had been good.

Then one day Clara had announced, solemnly, that they were no longer allowed to play together.

"My mother won't let me," said Clara. "She made me promise."

"Why?"

"Because of what you said about Sister Enda and Sister Barry."

"You told your mother?"

"I couldn't stop thinking about it. She said you were making things up."

"But I did see them." Jane had been on her way back from stowing the netballs after sports and taken a shortcut around the garden, which wasn't allowed, but she always went that way. The two nuns had been kissing. She'd seen it with her own eyes. Imagine. Sister Barry, with her hands dug into Sister Enda's hair, kneading around. "It's true."

"Even if it is . . ." but Clara had not known how to finish the sentence.

Jane wondered if Clara had also told her mother about Miss Banks—and then decided she had.

"You don't understand because you don't have a mother," said Clara calmly. "Mothers know things, even when you don't tell them."

But what things? It was horrendously unfair, and although this moratorium on their friendship clearly made Clara suffer, she was sticking to it.

Jane had climbed the tree alone. And it was dangerous. Even Jane, with her monkey ability, her confidence in placing hand on branch, swinging legs to place her foot in one spot and then quickly in the next without losing momentum, had moments of fear. But she kept going. The nest was up there. She'd seen the warbler flying back and forth, worm in beak. There had to be fledglings, and when she drew closer, she could hear them chirping hungrily. Here, above it all, she had a view of the grotto, of Sister Enda moving through the rows of vegetable garden, and over on playing fields, she could see girls racing each other on the track, skipping rope. Girls were playing house over by the bank of trees by the tennis courts. And there was Clara, with her red hair, talking to someone by the front gate, gesturing with her hands. The branch that led to the nest was broad and straight. You could grasp it with your knees and edge along. Of course, reaching a place was never as difficult as finding your way back, but—skirt tucked into the legs of her underwear—Jane managed. The mother bird flew quickly away, but Jane could see the tips of the baby birds' beaks stabbing into the air, so very hungry.

Clara had seen Jane in the tree, high in its branches. "There's a nest," Jane said. Jane saw the look of curiosity flicker across Clara's features. And during penmanship, Jane

scrawled across the top of Clara's notebook: *You're a baby.*
You'll never do it. Jane then waited at lunchtime at the base
of the tree, and sure enough Clara had joined her.

"Just this last time," she'd said, looking nervously
around.

And the two climbed, Jane first, showing Clara where
to place her feet, showing her that the impossible could be
managed until they were both in the realm of sky, like gods,
aloft, while all the other children remained earthbound.
Soon they were jammed into the fork of branches, and the
broad branch, the one with the nest, stretched out before
them. "The hardest bit is done now," Jane had said. "You
just have to crawl along."

"It's too hard," Clara said. "I can't do it."

"What do you mean you can't do it?"

"I'll never get back."

"You go first, then, so you can see how I turn around."

"I'm sweating. My palms are slippery." Clara wiped her
hands on her pinafore. "I don't have to do everything you
tell me to," which sounded parroted from her mother. "I can
say no."

And that's when Jane had lost patience. She had shoved
her, just a little, but Clara had been trying to reverse her
direction on the branch. Then suddenly she was gone and
the sound of snapping branches and whipping leaves was all
there was, until a thud and a crunching sound as Clara hit

the ground. Jane was unsure what had happened. It seemed impossible. But there was Sister Barry running across the lawn, and there was Clara. Her body was twisted in a way that seemed impossible, her shoulders moved in one way, her legs out to the side. No one could bend like that. Jane caught sight of Clara's face—her eyes wide with terror as she tried to breathe. Jane clambered out of the tree, tearing her pinafore on a branch, scraping her leg, and when she reached the ground, Clara was still breathing. *Call an ambulance*, was shouted by someone, but then Clara grew still, her eyes open, looking at nothing.

As Jane brushed her teeth, she looked down the hall with a sense of pained foreboding. She walked to her room, aware that she was retracing the steps of the whispering voice of the night before. How would she sleep? Even without the whispering, Sister Enda's tale of Sister Iona was bouncing around in her head. And Mrs. Glave, of the hair-brushing sister, was in the guest room snoring away, as Jane's father had been called to York for a trial. What if the sister was feeling missed again? Jane would sleep with the light on. Or better yet, she would stay awake until dawn. She was reading through the Famous Five books and was on to the third book in the series, *Five Run Away Together*. Clara had bought her the first one for her birthday, and now she felt compelled to read them all, because when she read them, it felt as though Clara were reading with her, as though nothing had gone wrong. The lights were on. She would last out the night.

Jane's eyes flew open to see the girl sitting on her bed. She must have fallen asleep. The girl had her back turned to her, and Jane realized that she must be dreaming. The girl's red hair was tangled with leaves and twigs, the uniform dirtied. It was Clara, but it could not be Clara, because Clara was gone. Jane, propped on the pillows, quietly watched her, and both were still, but then the girl began to move. She appeared to be struggling to stand, and then she did, but her back was twisted in an awkward way, her right hip pitched far to the left, her neck bent. Slowly the girl began to turn around, limping as she did, making a slow orbit. It was Clara, so pale that she was almost blue. Her lips were also blue, although darker, thin, and her eyes a lighter green than they had ever been, an unnatural yellowed color. Jane froze in place, hearing her heart thudding in her chest, unable to move.

"Jane," she said. "Jane." The voice labored, hissing through her constricted throat, struggling for breath. Clara reached out a hand to Jane, a hand that dangled limply on a snapped wrist. "Remember," she said. "Friends forever."

"I'm so sorry," Jane stammered. "I didn't mean to."

Clara smiled, but it was with no warmth. She began to move around the end of the bed, drawing closer, her step a limp and drag, her face filled with an awesome purpose.

Jane was aware of her screaming then, although she did not know how much time had passed. Mrs. Glave was at the door.

"Jane!" she shouted. "Jane!" And then she was holding Jane to her bosom, rocking her softly.

"Mrs. Glave," Jane whispered. "I had a dream."

"A dream? I saw her. I saw her bending over you. What does she want?"

Jane was crying and talking and shouting all at once. She pulled open the drawer of her bedside table and found the narrow braid of hair. "We were meant to be friends forever," Jane whimpered.

Mrs. Glave released Jane from her arms, her face composed in terror. "What is that?"

"We made a pact, Clara and I, and now—"

"You will take that thing from this house first thing tomorrow. And you will burn it." Mrs. Glave stepped back from the bed.

"But can't you—"

"I will not touch it. The devil is in that hair, and now that girl in his hands. She will not rest until you get rid of it."

"But can't you help me?"

"Oh, I have tried with you, Jane, but I will not traffic in the devil's work. You burn that first thing, or she'll be back."

*   *   *

There would be no sleep that night. Jane had dressed for school and waited in the kitchen through the last few hours of darkness as Mrs. Glave, rosary in hand, filled the remainder of the quiet night with her pleading whisper. When it was finally time for Jane to go to school, Mrs. Glave put on her good walking shoes and fixed her hair, placed Jane's lunch in her school case, and helped Jane with her hat, all as usual, but the routines failed to please, and Mrs. Glave was unable to offer any solace. They walked in silence to the school gates. "You know what you need to do," she said, placing her hands on Jane's shoulders.

Mr. Duggan had just done with the wastepaper baskets, and as the incinerator was at good heat, it was probably a good time to get the latest trimming from the hedges in there as well. He saw the girl standing at the trestle by the incinerator. She was the troublemaker, the one with the rich father they said had pushed her friend from the tree. And he had seen her lurking around the incinerator before. He was sure it was this girl with the black hair who had found his magazines where they'd been hidden by the milk crate. And now she was sneaking around the incinerator again. What was she up to? She looked nervous, peering over her shoulder, but she hadn't noticed him. If she was after his magazines again, she'd have no luck, because of course he'd found a new hiding place. The nuns were a bit odd and the pay could have been better, but it was a decent job and he planned to keep it. And there she was again, now whispering, but to who? And the look on her face. All right, there was something up, and maybe someone else was there, but he'd thought it was just the one child. They shouldn't have been playing by the incinerator. It wasn't safe. He set the rake down and was just making his way to impose some order when the girl opened the incinerator. She seemed to be trying to get something in there, something small, but was moving in this awkward way, as if she were wrestling with someone else. And then it happened. A flame licked out and caught the edge of her pinafore. Now he was running. "Roll," he shouted. "On the ground!"

But she screamed and threw her arms about. She crashed into the trestle and the dead weeds up against it, dry as hay, had roared to life. He took off his jacket and tried to smother the flames, but she was screaming and wouldn't stay still. By the time he managed to push her to the ground, she was horribly burned. He had seen injuries like this in the war. She'd make it through the night in hospital and be gone sometime the following day.

The police had asked Mr. Duggan if he knew what the girl was doing by the incinerator. He shrugged. The girls were not allowed there, so she must have been up to something. "Ah, don't ask me," he'd said. "You'd better ask that other girl, her friend. I saw her, just after this one caught on fire."

"What other girl?" asked Sister Barry. "What other girl?"

"All I can tell you," said Mr. Duggan, "is that she has red hair."